ULTIMATE ENDING

BOOK 4

ENIGMA
AT THE
GREENSBORO ZOO

Check out the full

ULTIMATE ENDING BOOKS

Series:

TREASURES OF THE FORGOTTEN CITY

THE HOUSE ON HOLLOW HILL

THE SHIP AT THE EDGE OF TIME

ENIGMA AT THE GREENSBORO ZOO

THE SECRET OF THE AURORA HOTEL

THE STRANGE PHYSICS OF THE HEIDELBERG LABORATORY

THE TOWER OF NEVER THERE

www.UltimateEndingBooks.com

Cover design by Milan Jaram www.MilanJaram.com

Internal artwork by Jaime Buckley www.jaimebuckley.com

Enjoyed this book? Please take the time to leave a review on Amazon.

Dedicated to Grace Gifford;
I've never seen a bluebird more loved.

Welcome to **Ultimate Ending**,
where YOU choose the story!

That's right – everything that happens in this book is a result of decisions YOU make. So choose wisely!

But also be careful. Throughout this book you'll find tricks and traps, trials and tribulations! Most you can avoid with common sense and a logical approach to problem solving. Others will require a little bit of luck. Having a coin handy, or a pair of dice, will make your adventure even more fun. So grab em' if you got em'!

Along the way you'll also find tips, clues, and even items that can help you in your quest. You'll meet people. Pick stuff up. Taking note of these things is often important, so while you're gathering your courage, you might also want to grab yourself a pencil and a sheet of paper.

Keep in mind, there are *many* ways to end the story. Some conclusions are good... some not so good.
Some of them are even great!
But remember:

There is only *ONE*

ULTIMATE ENDING!

ENIGMA AT THE GREENSBORO ZOO

Welcome to the Greensboro Zoo!

You are KATY RODRIGUEZ, a Corporal in the Greensboro City Police Department. Not only are you one of the city's finest in uniform, but you're the top candidate for promotion to Sergeant next month. You've been working hard, putting in the extra hours, and it's all finally about to pay off.

All you need to do is coast until then, and not screw up.

You leave the small convenience store with two coffees in hand, and climb into the driver side of your police cruiser. "Dude, you got me decaf, right?" asks JERRY HOLMAN, your patrol partner.

"Yes," you say, handing him his cup. He's a good policeman, but a bit of a old grouch. And he whines a lot.

"Two sugars, no cream," you add as he opens his mouth to ask. "And don't call me dude!"

His mouth closes and he nods thankfully. "Why are you drinking the strong stuff?" he asks, glancing at his watch. "We've only got an hour until shift's over."

"I'm hoping to catch the second half of the game," you say, testing the temperature of the coffee. The Greensboro Gryphons are two games from making the playoffs, and this will be one of the few nights you get home in time to see any of the game.

Jerry shrugs. "Me, I'm going to get some much needed sleep."

"All you do is sleep," you tease.

"Hey, some of us enjoy a rest. We can't all bust our butts to make Sergeant!"

You think of another joke, but bite it back. You *have* been busting your butt, and it's nice to hear someone say so.

Suddenly your radio crackles to life. "Unit 41. Unit 41. Come in."

Uh oh. That's you.

8

You move your coffee to your other hand and grab the radio receiver. "This is Unit 41, over."

"Please hold for Captain Beckett." The radio goes silent.

You share a look with Jerry. Captain Beckett? It's rare for one of the station chiefs to get on the dispatch radio.

The speaker hisses with static before the Captain's voice sounds. "Officer Rodriguez? Officer Holman?"

"We're here, Captain."

"Good, good, uhh..." he pauses to take a deep breath. "There's a disturbance at the Greensboro City Zoo. I need you to take a look."

Jerry groans.

"Sir," you say, "we're six miles from there. Surely there's a patrol that's closer."

"I trust you with this, Rodriguez," he says gruffly. "Are you saying you can't handle it?"

"Of course not, sir," you quickly say. "What kind of disturbance?"

There's a long silence on the radio. "Our details are fuzzy. They'll tell you when you get there."

"*But we get off in an hour,*" Jerry whispers.

You hold a finger up to shush him. "Roger that, Captain."

"I'm counting on you, Rodriguez," Captain Beckett says ominously. The radio goes dead.

You and Jerry sit there for a few quiet moments.

"There goes my extra sleep," Jerry mutters.

"Oh quit whining," you say. "We'll pop over there and take care of it in a pinch."

Jerry takes the coffee from your hand. "Well then you'd better give *me* the strong stuff."

9

The police siren wails and flashes as you wind through the city. Five minutes later you're whizzing past the "Welcome to the Greensboro City Zoo" sign and screeching to a stop in the parking lot.

You and Jerry climb out of the car simultaneously. Although it's well past the zoo's closing hours, the massive metal gates stand wide open. A few pieces of paper blow through the opening.

"That's weird," Jerry says.

You nod. You've got a strange feeling about this.

Your boots crunch along the pavement as you approach. A flock of colorful birds flutter into the air as you pass through the gates and into the zoo walkway, but nothing scarier than that.

Ahead of you is the Visitor Center, where tickets and souvenirs are sold. There's some sort of red light on inside the window. A shadow passes in front of it.

Involuntarily, your hand touches your pistol holster. "Who's there!" you call out. "This is the Greensboro Police Department!"

The man steps out from the building. In the moonlight you see that he's young, like an intern, wearing a zoo uniform with green suspenders. "Oh thank goodness you're here," he says, frantic. "I'm not cut out for this. *Way* above my skill level."

You relax. "Calm down. Can you tell us what's going on?"

"I've gotta get out of here," he says, pushing past you.

"Hey, wait!" Jerry yells as the intern makes a break for the entrance.

"You're safe with us," you add. "We're trained officers with weapons."

"You're going to need more than that!" the intern yells. "There's tranquilizer rifles in the Warden's Hut, if you can get there!" And with that he disappears into the darkness.

You glance at Jerry. He's too stunned to speak.

10

The lights are off in the Visitor Center, and you realize that reddish glow was an emergency light over the doorway. "Looks like the power is out," you say.

Jerry points. "The door to the employee office is in the corner."

You head over to the door, which has, "Employees Only" printed in big yellow letters. There's an electronic keypad next to the door, with numbers 1-9 glowing. There must be a backup generator to keep the emergency systems online.

Thankfully the door is wide open, so you slip inside.

There are desks and file cabinets filled with papers. The only illumination comes from another emergency light above the doorway, and a single computer screen across the room.

Jerry grabs a medical kit from the desk. "Why's that computer on?"

"Must be on the backup circuit," you say, stepping up to it. There's an email open:

Jeremy, as the only member of the night crew it's imperative that you get the systems back online. Get to the Maintenance Shed and enable the backup power. If you need protection from Project Fusion then retrieve a tranq rifle from the Warden Hut. You know the code.

-Warden Oxford

And a response:

Respectfully, sir: you're out of your mind! I'm not trained for that kind of work, and it would only make her ANGRY! I've called the police. Let them take care of it. I'm getting out of here.

-Jeremy

"Huh," Jerry says after reading. "What's Project Fusion?"

You shake your head. "I don't know, but it sounds dangerous. It's a good thing you grabbed that medical kit. We'd better call the Captain."

Call for backup *ON PAGE 14*

11

The path through the woods winds around the side of the Insect Enclosure. It's clear that the zoo has been meticulously landscaped to give a certain wilderness feel. Jungle fronds the size of surf boards hang down over the path, blocking much of your view. You're forced to push them aside with one hand while holding your flashlight with the other.

A rain begins falling, pattering against the enormous leaves. "Maybe inside would have been better," you say.

"Dude..." Jerry mutters, pointing up at the building. "I don't think so."

Up on the roof of the Insect Enclosure, just above the second floor, is an enormous hole. It's the size of a small car, with claw marks on the side. It looks like Wolverine ripped his way free!

"I guess it's a good thing we didn't go up there, huh?" Jerry says.

You give the hole one final look before turning away. "I guess so."

"Do you think it was that Project Fusion, or whatever?"

You shake your head in wonder. "I don't know *what* could cause something like that, but Project Fusion sure sounds crazy enough. Maybe we can find more information about it in the park."

"Maybe."

Continue along the path *ON PAGE 30*

12

It should have been obvious, you realize. Droppings everywhere, and those strange dark objects on the ceiling blocking the glass.

Jerry and you raise your eyes to the ceiling as one. Up there, among the metal rafters, are birds.

Hundreds of birds.

Jerry swallows audibly. "Well as long as they stay up there..."

Three birds jump off their perches and begin circling the ceiling, a hundred feet above you. Their wings are incredibly wide, like surfboards.

"Stay calm," you say. "We're going to quietly walk to the exit and–"

One of the birds pulls its wings close to its body. It's diving toward you.

"Run!"

Jerry takes off, with you close behind. The birds above begin to screech. You get halfway to the exit when you realize you're not going to make it. The bird is growing fast, wind whipping at its dark feathers. You're going to have to throw yourself to the ground to avoid it. And it will be there any second.

FLIP TWO COINS! How many times did it land heads?

If it landed heads 0 times, *GO TO PAGE 58*
If it landed heads 1 time, *GO TO PAGE 37*
If it landed heads 2 times, *GO TO PAGE 20*

13

At the center of the observation area is a ring of railing, keeping people from falling down inside the animal area. You walk all around the railing, searching the knocked over tables and other debris all around. There's nothing there that can help you, just a bunch of junk: a Greensboro Gryphons jersey, some empty food wrappers, and a plastic bag blowing across the floor.

You step up to the railing and look down inside the pit. It's a mostly grassy enclosure, with a small lake down on the left and several wooden logs scattered about. At one end is a dark cave that leads somewhere deeper inside.

Something shiny catches your attention. You squint down and see a golden coin sitting on one of the logs.

The Tower Token!

You take stock of the area. The railing only comes up to your chest, so you should be able to jump over... but then it's a twenty foot drop to the ground. And once down there, how will you get out?

But getting that token seems important. You lift your foot and prepare to jump over.

"Hey!" Jerry suddenly calls out. "Check this out!"

Follow his voice *OVER TO PAGE 66*

14

The phones are down–which is probably why the intern used email to communicate–but thankfully you've got your radio. "Dispatch, this is officer Rodriguez, over."

A few minutes later and you're connected to the Captain. "Huh?" he asks.

"Sir, the place is deserted. The only night employee just ran away like he'd seen a ghost! The power is out too." You quickly fill him in on the details of the email.

Captain Beckett clears his throat when you finish. "Well..."

Suddenly there is a rumble outside. You and Jerry run to the window just in time to see a huge, hulking shape. As it comes into view the moonlight glistens off two long, ivory tusks.

An elephant!

15

You watch in stunned silence as it lumbers past and walks out the gate, into the street. "Duuude..." whispers Jerry.

"And I think the animals are loose," you add to the radio. "I'm officially requesting backup. We need animal control in here."

The Captain sighs. "Okay, I'm going to be straight with you, Rodriguez. Warden Oxford is an old friend of mine, and he needs our help. We've already contacted animal control, but they won't be there for two hours. I need to you to do whatever cleanup you can until then. Try to contain as many of the animals as possible. And close those gates, so no more animals get out! I don't know why the power is out, but figure it out."

"But sir, we're not qualified for this sort of thing."

"If you take care of this," he adds, "that promotion is as good as yours. If you don't... well. Carry on then. And oh, make sure you don't harm any of the animals."

"What?" Jerry blurts out.

"I'm serious, Holman. Lock your sidearm in the police cruiser, so you're not tempted to use it. Injured animals are a PR nightmare. Understood?"

"Yessir."

The radio goes silent.

"Well then." You unholster your sidearm and hand it to Jerry. "Put 'em away."

He stares, dumbfounded. "You can't be serious."

"It was a direct order. We still have our pepper spray. Go ahead, I'll stay here and look around."

After he grumbles and heads back to the car, you look around the Visitor Center. There's a stack of maps on the check-out counter, but they're all shredded. Knowing what's going on in the Zoo, a beaver probably chewed them up.

"I'm sure we have a lot of ground to cover," you tell Jerry when he gets back. "And a *lot* of animals to wrangle. Let's get to it."

Head into the zoo grounds *ON PAGE 18*

16

Despite the chaos of the Monkey Manor, the office is the cleanest one you've seen yet. There's a tidy computer desk with stacks of papers in a bin.

You pick up the first sheet of paper.

ZOO ANNOUNCEMENT.

Dave, I'm serious. Stop messing around in the Power Station. I know you think it's funny to reverse the order of the power circuits, but enough is enough. Carl got zapped last week. If it happens again I'm going to assign you back to cleaning the cages for Project Fusion.

-Warden Oxford

"No code here," you say. "Any luck over there?"

Jerry sifts through the stack of papers. "Nope. Well, not for the Power Station, at least. I did find the code to the Bird Bastion."

He hands you a plastic card with indented lettering on it:

BIRD BASTION CODE: 105

You search the rest of the room. There's nothing else useful. "Well I guess we'd better go check the Bird Bastion then," you say with a sigh.

Sliding back outside, you hold the banana out in front of you. The monkeys along the porch fence stare intently, heads slowly following you. Tossing it through the hole, you make a run for the path.

Head back to the Power Station *ON PAGE 47*

17

"Jerry, I could really use your help on this."

He doesn't budge. "You've got it, partner. I trust you."

"Jerry..."

"Just guess something! You've got a 50-50 shot."

King Snake sounds the most dangerous, so you select that answer on the screen. The podium flashes red and makes a sound that obviously is meant to signal defeat.

"Aww, man." You sigh and walk back to Jerry. "I guessed wrong."

He's not even paying attention, still darting his head from one glass tank to the other. "Can we just get out of here now? Please?"

"Fine."

Return to the tower *ON PAGE 154*

18

You pass through the turnstiles and into the zoo grounds. With the power off, the path that winds through the park is dark and ominous. You pull out your flashlight and cast a cone of light before you. With the way the shadows play you're still unnerved, and the fingers of your free hand itch to grab the pepper spray from your belt. Jerry is unusually quiet, so he must feel the same.

To steady yourself, you stop to read one of the informational signs along the path:

*When defending yourself from a bear attack, the species of bear will determine the best course of action. If attacked by a **Black Bear**, fight back by striking the bear in the head and face. **Grizzly Bears** are not so timid, however, so the best course of action is to fall to the ground in the fetal position and play dead.*

Jerry is stopped at the next sign ahead of you, doing the same. That one is about snakes:

*The **Coral Snake** and **King Snake** look similar, but don't be fooled! **Coral Snakes** are venomous, while **King Snakes** are harmless. To remember the difference, say the rhyme: If red touches black, it's safe for Jack. If red touches yellow, it kills the fellow.*

Jerry swallows audibly. "We're not going to have to deal with snakes, are we?"

"I don't know."

"Because I'm not a biologist, or a snakeologist, or whatever it's called that–"

You cut him off. "Come on. Let's keep moving. The path splits up ahead."

19

The sound of splashing water greets you as you enter a wide pavilion. In the center is a stone fountain spraying water over the edge. The falling mist looks strange in the light of your flashlight. "But if the electricity is out," you say, "then what's powering the pump?"

Jerry points. "I don't think that's the pump causing that..."

Without warning, a brown antelope leaps out of the fountain. It lands on the ground and teeters on unsteady legs, the hooves slipping wetly on the pavement. When it regains its balance it stares directly at you, flicks its ears, and then bolts.

Three more antelope bound out of the fountain to follow, leaving a trail of water leading into the woods. The sound of rustling trees slowly fades.

"Well," you say, "it's better than snakes. Right?"

Jerry mumbles something incoherent.

You approach the fountain. Rising out of the center is a signpost with ten arrows pointing in different directions. "The Warden's email said we need to turn the power on."

"It also said," Jerry points out, "that we should grab tranquilizer rifles from the Warden Hut if we need protection from Project Fusion."

"We don't even know what Project Fusion is."

Jerry nods vigorously. "Exactly!"

The arrow for the Maintenance Shed points to the left. The arrow for the Warden Hut points to the right.

What's the plan, officer?

To turn on the power, *FLIP TO PAGE 27*
If you would rather get a better weapon, *GO TO PAGE 38*

20

You try to time it right, but the bird zips through the air impossibly fast. You throw yourself flat but it's too late. The bird spreads its massive wings at the last moment and pulls up, feet full of talons outstretched.

Fire rips across your back as you land on the ground in the bird droppings. You feel feathers beating furiously past your hair, like a leaf blower on the back of your head.

"Rodriguez!" Jerry yells.

He comes running as you groan, reaching behind you to touch your back. It stings. "Let's get out of here," Jerry says.

He tries to pull you to your feet, but you're too dazed. "What was that thing," you say.

"It was a hawk, I think. Come on Rodriguez, we have to go!" He looks up. "Oh. Oh no..."

You follow his gaze and see a dark shape high in the sky. It's getting bigger. You realize that's because it's diving again. *I always hated birds*, you think to yourself as you watch it near. And now you hate them more, because this one is responsible for...

THE END

21

You follow the path for a while and come to another building. "The Insect Enclosure," Jerry reads. He gives a shiver. "I hate bugs."

"Is there anything you *do* like?" you ask.

"I like to sleep," he mutters.

You shine your flashlight at the building. Everything looks fine there. Or you could continue down the path in the direction of the Warden Hut.

Check inside the Insect Enclosure *ON PAGE 26*
If you want to stay on the path, *GO TO PAGE 11*

22

"We can't risk injuring any of the animals," you decide, "and we can't risk our own lives."

"Then what do we do?"

There's another door to the left, with an emergency light overhead. "Follow me!"

You burst through the door before the stampeding sound can reach you. You're in a small employee hallway now, with offices on either side and an exit sign dead ahead. You run down the hall and throw your shoulder into the door, which dumps you outside.

Now you're in a small dirt path between buildings. Another, smaller structure is straight ahead. A sign next to the door says, "Insect Enclosure."

A strange screech cuts through the air.

It sounds like a bird, but deeper. More animal. You both freeze and wait as it fades.

"That was a few hundred feet that way," Jerry says, pointing.

Still not feeling completely safe, you dart toward the Insect Enclosure and test the door. It opens.

"Come on, in here!"

Enter the building *ON PAGE 26*

23

The hippo is close, practically stepping on the backs of your feet. It's time to show that famous Greensboro City Police Academy training! Hoping your timing is good, you turn to the right and throw your upper body forward, ducking your head down toward your chest.

You roll across the mud and feel the hippo rush past you, narrowly missing.

Jumping to your feet, you sprint the rest of the way toward the building. It looks like an open structure, sort of like a barn, but it has a door and that's all that matters. The hippo recovers from missing you and begins chasing again, but you've bought yourself enough time. You slide through the open door and quickly pull it shut.

Nice! See what happens next *ON PAGE 71*

24

"Too bad we don't have the keycode," you sigh. "Up the ladder we go."

You follow Jerry around the side. The ladder is bolted into the cement and leads to the roof of the Warden Hut, maybe thirty feet above. There's no moonlight now, so the ladder is completely dark.

Jerry notices you hesitating. "Hey, you're the one who decided to get the tranquilizer darts before turning on the power."

Thinking of the promotion Captain Beckett promised, you grab the closest rung of the ladder and start climbing. You can't see anything but your hands and feet slowly move from one rung to another.

When you're halfway up the ladder you feel Jerry start following. Your boots on the metal make banging noises in the night. You wonder if this is what burglars feel like, scaling a building in the dark.

There's a weird rattling sound. Like metal scraping in a way it's not supposed to.

You stop and squint into the darkness.

The ladder is bolted into the cement in front of you. Or at least it should be–you realize the bolt has come loose. With each step Jerry takes the ladder slides farther and farther out of its securing.

"Jerry," you say. "The ladder's loose up here. Jump off and wait until I'm up."

"Dude, I'm way too high," he says. "It's at least fifteen feet down. Just keep going. You're almost to the top, right?"

The gap between the ladder and wall is quickly growing. You open your mouth to tell Jerry to hurry down.

The ladder comes loose.

25

The ladder falls backwards, throwing you into the air. Butterflies blossom in your stomach for an instant before you crash into the ground. You roll as you land, coming up safe.

"Whew. That was a close one. Jerry?"

He's on the ground groaning. You rush over and see that his ankle is bent in the wrong direction. "Sorry Rodriguez," he hisses through clenched teeth. "Should have... listened."

You call in Jerry's injury to the station. Captain Beckett reluctantly tells you to sit tight and wait for animal control. You can tell he's disappointed. Maybe you'll get the promotion another time, but for now it's not looking good.

"Guess we should have turned the lights on first," Jerry says.

"Or found the code to get into the Warden Hut the safe way," you mutter.

He smiles at you gratefully.

It could have been worse, you suppose. You've run into a lot of dangerous animals. It's probably for the best that animal control is taking over. But you still wish you could have figured out what Project Fusion was. Maybe you'll have another chance, when it isn't...

THE END

26

You're in a big, open room with glass cages covering every wall. It looks like an aquarium store, except you know these aren't fish. "It doesn't look like there's any damage in here," you say.

"Thank goodness for that!" Jerry gives an exaggerated shiver to let you know what he thinks about bugs.

You walk along one wall, reading off different types of insects. *Orthoptera Caelifera*, or the the common grasshopper. Next to that are some locusts and katydids, which look like they have longer antenna. Everything seems really calm and creepy under the glow of the emergency lights.

There's a piece of paper on the ground. You pick it up. It looks like a handwritten note from one employee to another:

Sarah,

Starting this week the lions in the Safari Sanctum are going to be fed only steak. No more fish! They've been moody lately and are sick of fish, and won't eat it at all. I know you guys need more fish for that secret project of yours, so I'm sure you'll be happy for the extra.

-Jessica

You're about to show it to Jerry when you hear his voice.

"Hey Rodriguez," he calls from another room. "Come check this out."

See what Jerry's found *ON PAGE 28*

27

"There's no use getting tranquilizer rifles if we can't see what we're shooting," you decide. "Besides, walking around a dark zoo gives me the creeps. Let's work on turning the power back on first."

Jerry grumbles but doesn't argue further.

You follow the sign toward the west side of the park. On either side of the paved path are nicely manicured bushes and flowers. You haven't been to the zoo in years, but it seems like it would be a nice place to visit. In other circumstances, of course.

There's a rumble in the sky. "Hope it doesn't rain on us."

"Yeah," you agree.

"Hey," Jerry adds. "Check this out."

His flashlight is aimed off the path, to a section of the grass between the path and some trees. There's something strange in the ground. You leave the path and approach, and find a small keycard with words:

POWER STATION CODE: 132

"I meant that," he says, pointing. You follow his gaze and realize there are footprints in the mud.

Enormous animal footprints.

"They look like paws," Jerry says.

"Yeah, but have you ever seen anything with paws that big?" They're as big as a volleyball!

"I don't know." Jerry begins looking around the woods nervously.

You can tell he's a few minutes away from running back to your police cruiser. "Come on," you say. "There's the sign for the Power Station. It's just ahead."

Continue toward the power station *ON PAGE 33*

28

You follow his voice into a dark corridor. Jerry is standing at the base of a staircase that leads around a corner to the second floor. His flashlight shows a sign on the wall, but part of it has been scratched away by massive claws:

_________ *EXHIBIT, FLOOR TWO.*

"So much for not having any damage in here," you mutter.

"Well at least we saw this early, so we can avoid it," Jerry says. "Let's get out of here."

You shake your head. "We're supposed to contain all the animals until help arrives."

Jerry's jaw drops. "You can't be serious. Look at the claw marks!"

"I see them." They terrify you, wondering what could cause that, but you're no stranger to fear. "We have a job do to."

"Look," Jerry says, "I know you're the Corporal, but I think this is a really bad idea. We should get some tranquilizer guns first, like the Warden said. Be smart!" His face is pallid.

To see what's upstairs, *TURN TO PAGE 53*
To find your way outside, *GO TO PAGE 35*

29

"Let's see what's in the freezer," you say.

It's a massive industrial one, stainless steel and as big as a pickup truck. A burst of cold air and mist hits you in the face as you open it. Plastic trays full of food greet you: rows of steak, bottles of liquid, and every sized fish you could imagine.

Closing the door, you see a note taped on the side of the freezer.

ZOO ANNOUNCEMENT.

All Penguin Palace feeding rations are to be cut by 10% until further notice. Another project at the zoo has taken priority, and we're nearly out of our supply of fish. Don't like it? Complain to the supply chief.

-Warden Oxford

"Another project," you mutter. "Sounds like that Project Fusion we read about."

"Whatever it is, it eats fish," Jerry says. "That could be a lot of things."

There's something else on the counter. It looks like a credit card, with words indented on its face:

SNAKE SANCTUARY CODE: 119

You pocket the card. "This'll come in handy if we see the Snake Sanctuary later."

Jerry shivers.

There's nothing else around there worth looking at. "Okay, let's try the Pantry."

Open the Pantry *ON PAGE 34*

30

You round a corner down the path, not paying attention. Without warning the paved path becomes mud. Worse, it's beginning to slope downward.

You halt yourself just in time to see a long, wet mud slide. Whew! That would have been bad if–

Not realizing you've stopped, Jerry bumps into your back.

For a brief moment you're flying forward, arms stretched out like Superman. Then you hit the mud and you're sliding, limbs flailing all around to try and slow yourself. The water and mud rubs against your chin and chest, flying into your mouth and eyes. Your fingers grab some grass on the bank but it rips loose.

Splash. You're fully submerged in water, like being dunked in a dark swimming pool. You bob to the surface and gasp for air. You hear a distant screaming voice draw closer, and then Jerry's body splashes into the water next to you. A cone of light slides down the hill after him before joining you both in the water.

You grab the flashlight, glad that it's waterproof. "You okay?" you ask as Jerry treads water.

"Why'd you stop!"

You wave a hand at the hill. "Maybe because there's a *giant mudslide on the path?* Why did *you* knock me down?"

"It's not my fault," he mumbles.

You cock your ears. The rain is still pattering in the trees above, but you don't hear anything else. "Hopefully nothing heard us," you say.

Jerry groans. "Let's just get out of here."

31

The water only comes up to your waist, allowing you to wade through it somewhat easily. Jerry leads the way with the flashlight, grumbling about how his best uniform is now ruined. You consider reminding him that it's his fault but decide to bite your tongue.

Jerry yelps. "Ahh!"

"What's wrong?"

The light from the flashlight waves all around the air like a spotlight as he frantically swipes at his arms. "Get them off!"

"Get *what* off?"

He's too panicked to answer, so you slosh forward to meet him. Dodging flailing arms, you grab the flashlight and shine it on him. "They're huge!" he cries, thrusting out his wrist.

It takes you a moment to recognize what they are. "Oh geez, Jerry," you say. "They're just leeches."

"You act like that's a relief!" He's practically terrified.

Reaching forward, you pluck a fat leech off his wrist. It comes away easily, but leaves a red splotch behind. "They're harmless," you explain.

"How do you know that!"

"Because I know," you reply, removing two more. They'd gotten up his sleeve. Even after getting them all off Jerry seems mortified. "Calm down. You're fine now."

"Hey," he says. "Do you feel that?"

"What?"

He pauses. "I think... I think the water is moving."

"It's just the waves from when I came running," you say. "I thought you were being attacked by something *real*."

Jerry shakes his head. "No. There's something else. It's definitely moving, can't you tell?"

You're about to make a joke about Jerry peeing his pants when you realize he's right. The water *is* moving. But what could cause that? You lick your lips and turn towards it.

Find out what's in the water *ON PAGE 48*

32

The hippo is close, practically stepping on the backs of your feet. It's time to show that famous Greensboro City Police Academy training! Hoping your timing is right, you turn to the right and throw your upper body forward, ducking your head down toward your chest.

You roll across the mud and feel the hippo rush past you, narrowly missing.

Using your hands to push yourself back up, you try to run–except you realize your foot is now stuck in some deep mud! Your foot must have fallen is some weird mud-filled hole, because it's covered almost to the knee. It's stuck!

The hippo slows a short distance away and turns around.

"Come on," you mutter, trying to pry your leg free. Down at the bottom you feel your shoe come off, but that doesn't help much. "Come on!"

The hippo sees you and begins another charge.

It's a way you never expected a police officer to go: run over by a hippopotamus while stuck in the mud. If you manage to survive you'll probably be the butt of jokes for the rest of your career. But in either case, as two tons of grey pachyderm comes bearing down on you, this will sadly be...

THE END

33

A chain-link fence with coils of barbed wire on the top appears ahead of you. Beyond that is a cement building partially sunk into the ground. A tall metal-framed tower rises above it, with power lines connecting to the top. If this isn't the Power Station, you don't know what is.

There's a signpost next to the gate, with three paths leading away: the Food Forest along the first path, the Monkey Manor down the middle one, and the Bird Bastion toward the lowest path.

Despite the imposing looking fence, the gate to the Power Station opens easily with a latch. "I thought it'd be tougher than that," Jerry says.

"Me too." You approach the building. Up close you can see that a tree branch has fallen across one of the power lines, ripping it loose. That's probably the cause of all the problems.

"How are we supposed to fix that?" Jerry asks.

"We shouldn't need to. The Warden's email said to restore backup power."

There's a set of cement steps sunken into the ground, leading to the front door. You hop down to the door and try the handle.

It doesn't budge. An electronic screen next to the door flashes: "Keycode required." There's a number pad underneath.

"So much for that," Jerry mutters.

Consider your options *ON PAGE 47*

34

It's a walk-in pantry, with shelves on either side extending away from you. There's bags of pasta, sacks of rice and beans, and pre-packaged foods like potato chips and candy bars. All the sorts of stuff they'd sell at the food court.

A quick glance around proves there's nothing interesting inside. "So much for that," you say.

Jerry grabs two bananas off the shelf as you leave. "Hey," you say. "We're here to help, not steal."

"It's just two bananas," Jerry protests. "Besides, I'm starving. All this running around has lowered my blood sugar. I would pay for it if I had cash!"

You pull out a one dollar bill from your pocket and stuff it on the counter where the bananas were. "You owe me," you say.

"Yeah, yeah."

YOU NOW HAVE TWO BANANAS!

Head back to the Power Station *ON PAGE 47*

35

"You're right," you admit. "Let's be safe. Come on, I think the other exit is this way."

You follow the hallway past a series of caterpillars and worms and other harmless things. You pass a map on the wall, which indicates that the second floor is devoted entirely to arachnids. Whew, good thing you didn't go up there!

Your flashlight passes over a small podium along one wall. A bright green sign says: "Trivia booth! Win a token to the Observation Tower!" To your surprise, the computer screen is glowing.

"Huh. I guess they put this on the emergency power circuit by mistake."

Glancing at the screen, it appears to be a series of trivia questions. The one on the screen currently says:

What common North American insect goes by the name Orthoptera Caelifera?

"The grasshopper!" you say.

Jerry wrinkles his face. "How'd you know that?"

"I'm smarter than you." After a moment you add, "And I just saw it on a display in the other room."

You select the grasshopper from the list of possible answers. A celebratory fanfare of horns blares out of a speaker in the podium and a small gold coin rolls out.

You pick it up and examine it beneath your flashlight. "Observation Tower," you read, the letters printed around the outside of the coin.

"That's the tower at the center of the zoo," Jerry says.

"Maybe some other time," you say. "When we're here to have fun. Come on, I think I see the employee office over there."

YOU NOW HAVE THE TOWER TOKEN!

Enter the office by *FLIPPING TO PAGE 77*

36

You didn't get this far in the police force by splitting up with your partner. Sending a final, furtive look toward the building ahead, you turn to follow Jerry.

The hippo follows.

"Jerry!" you call, not caring what else hears you in the open field. It would be pointless for him to slow down–there's no way for him to help against the hippo–but at the very least calling his name lets him know you're following. "Jerry!"

You look over your shoulder. The hippo is rumbling along, shaking the ground with each heavy step. And it's still gaining on you.

When you turn back around Jerry's nowhere to be seen. Did he run into the forest to the left? He couldn't have done it that fast.

And you're almost out of time.

There's a tree coming up, standing alone in the middle of the field. It's your only chance. There's a low branch you can grab... if you time it just right.

FLIP A COIN!

If heads, *RUN TO PAGE 94*
If tails, *JUMP OVER TO PAGE 39*

37

The bird is moving impossibly fast. Just before it reaches you, right as it extends its talons, you throw yourself onto the disgusting floor.

The air behind you rushes over you quickly, and for a moment you feel victorious. But then the paper with the Power Station code is ripped from your hands.

"Hey!"

You stare up and see a brown hawk flying away from you. In its talons is the sheet of paper. It flaps up toward the ceiling and perches on the rafters.

The other birds take this as a sign that the threat is over. They return to the rafters as well and calmly begin cleaning their feathers.

You and Jerry take the opportunity to finish running to the exit. You slip outside and close the door behind you.

"He took the code!" you tell Jerry.

"Yeah, I saw. Do you remember the riddle?" You shake your head. "Yeah, me neither."

"So what do we do?"

"I guess we head back to the path. We can go get the tranquilizer rifles at the Warden Hut..."

You look up at the Bird Bastion. There's a window in the glass high above, near the top. And right now it's open.

Jerry frowns. "You're not thinking about..."

The window is right next to the scaffolding the cleaners used. You could reach it by climbing the ladders.

"Rodriguez, *please* tell me you're not thinking of climbing up there."

To try getting the code, *CLIMB TO PAGE 44*

To heed Jerry's advice and make for the Warden Hut, *GO TO PAGE 21*

38

You don't like the sound of Project Fusion, and like being unprepared even less. "Tranq rifles it is," you say, turning to the right.

Jerry nods as if there were no other option.

The openness of the fountain pavilion disappears and the path becomes narrow and winding, with tall trees crowding all around. It feels like you're in the middle of the forest, except for the paved path. They've designed the zoo park well.

"The Warden Hut is on the other side of the park," Jerry says. "We've got a long way to go."

You reply, "Captain Beckett wants us to contain as many of the animals as we can. This will give us a chance to see some of the park."

The path split again. One way ends at a large building, and the other way..."

"Uh oh," Jerry says.

You shine your light in that direction. A massive oak tree has fallen across the path, blocking your way. At its base, where it snapped, large claw marks are raked into the bark.

"We can climb around," you suggest.

"No way," Jerry says. "What do you think knocked that down? Whatever it was, it was *big*."

You glance at the building. You don't see a sign anywhere to indicate what it is. "Okay then. Let's take a shortcut."

Enter the building *ON PAGE 43*

39

The tree is drawing near. You've got a twenty foot lead on the hippo, so if you time it right you should be able to scamper up a branch and into safety.

Ten steps. Five. Zero.

You leap with all your strength, your fingers slapping against the branch. Your fingers stick! A boot scrapes against the trunk and you pull yourself up. Although you think you're safe, you quickly reach for the next branch to put more distance between yourself and the pachyderm.

THWACK.

The entire tree is shaken just before you grab the next branch. Without a grip your feet slip on the wet branch and suddenly you're falling. Your back slams into the wood, you roll, and then plummet the rest of the way to the ground.

Even though the mud is wet, the force of landing knocks the wind from your lungs.

Groaning, you roll over and try to move. You can hear the hippo a short distance away. Is it coming back? You're not sure, and it hurts too much to look.

Just trying to take a tiny breath sends a sharp pain running across your chest. You've never had it happen, but based on the basic training you had you diagnose it as a broken rib. Maybe two. *Jerry's gunna laugh,* you think. *Falling out of a stupid tree.*

But Jerry's the least of your worries. As you finally muster the strength to look up you see something large and gray stumbling across the ground. The hippo, coming back around for another charge. Ahh, well. You suppose this isn't too bad of a way to go, but in any case it's still...

THE END

40

You've taken enough risks, and that growling noise has you spooked. "Yeah, I'm okay," you call back down to Jerry as you begin your descent.

He waits until you reach the ground. "What happened?"

"I came to my senses."

"You mean you listened to your partner, the honorable Officer Holman!"

You look around. "That sign over there says the Warden Hut is close," you say. "Let's go get those tranquilizer rifles. We should have done that from the start."

"Now you're speaking my language."

Despite what the sign says, the Warden Hut isn't very close. In fact, as the two of you make your way across the zoo you begin to wonder if you're lost. But then you see another sign for the Warden Hut that takes you down a new path.

You're almost there when a rumble drifts through the trees. You freeze, listening. "Sounds like... a swarm of flies," Jerry says.

"Those are some big flies," you say skeptically. "That's more like a stampede of gazelles!"

You both remove your pepper spray at the same time. The sound is coming to the south, down a winding path. Whatever it is, it's coming your way. You share a look with Jerry and prepare to defend yourselves.

A light appears in the distance. You begin to relax as you realize what the sound was.

Three black, windowless vans round a corner and pull up next to you on the path. Men with "Animal Control" printed on their uniforms hop to the ground and begin fanning out. One man dressed differently climbs out of the front jeep. The headlights from the vehicle blind you until he comes close.

"Captain!" Jerry immediately salutes.

41

Captain Beckett is a bull of a man, sixty years old with broad shoulders and muscular arms. His uniform is tight and orderly, his face chiseled with discipline.

You follow Jerry's example and salute, feeling dazed. "Captain, we didn't expect you for a while longer. We were still gaining control of the park."

"Were you, Corporal?" he asks. "Because from the looks of things you haven't gained control of anything at all. Status report, pronto."

You lick your lips nervously. "Sir. We have secured the Food Forest, Monkey Manor, and Bird Bastion. We did our best to restore power to the zoo, but the codes to the Power Station have been manipulated. By some employee named Dave."

"I knew it was Dave's fault," says a new voice. A young man wearing a Greensboro City Zoo uniform. "He's been playing jokes for weeks. I swear, if I find him I'm going to jerk a knot in his tail..."

Jerry clears his throat. "Are you Warden Oxford?"

The man laughs. "Heavens no! Do I sound like I have an English accent?" He doesn't. "Oxford is over at the Warden Hut arming himself to the teeth. They're going to need everything they've got to bring down..." he trails off.

"To bring down Project Fusion?" Jerry blurts.

The zoo employee tenses. "What do you know about that?"

"Nothing," you quickly say. "We've just seen Zoo Announcements about it."

The employee stares at you for a long moment before nodding. "Be glad for that. If you had come across her... no matter. Captain. Thank you for your assistance. These fine officers have done a wonderful job." He walks away.

You beam, until the Captain says, "Don't look so smug. He might be happy that you've secured three areas, but I had hoped for more. I expected better of you, Rodriguez."

"Does this mean I won't be promoted..."

"We will see." And with that he turns and walks away too.

You glance at Jerry and shrug. It could have been worse. You may not get that promotion, but you did your best. And you're walking out of the Greensboro City Zoo alive. You still wonder what Project Fusion is, but that's something you'll have to figure out another time...

THE END

42

"There's no way we can reach the employee office through *that*," you decide.

Jerry smirks. "Afraid of getting your uniform messy?"

Right on cue, a wet piece of monkey dung bounces off Jerry's chest. The horrified look on his face is priceless. The monkeys shriek and scream with delight.

"Too late, eh partner?"

"Let's just go," he grumbles.

Head back to the Power Station *AT PAGE 47*

43

Red emergency lights guide you into the entrance of the building. A blast of cold air hits you in the face. It's *freezing* in here!

"Brrrr," Jerry says.

There's a podium and computer in the center of the entranceway, where an employee would stand and direct people. You walk behind and look around. A formal looking notice is sitting next to the keyboard:

ZOO ANNOUNCEMENT.

There have been a lot of questions from zoo staff about Project Fusion. Please be advised that only biologists directly involved with the project are permitted in the lab. Anyone else will be terminated immediately.

-Warden Oxford

"Find anything?" Jerry asks.

You shake your head. No need to keep scaring him.

The two of you head farther down the hallway, where one entire wall is made of glass. Some sort of half-aquarium is inside, with rocks and water. Ahead of you is an employee door, broken off its hinges and part of the wall ripped loose.

"That looks bad," you admit.

Jerry just stares, wide-eyed.

Suddenly there's a rumbling sound. A tiny tremble in the ground, felt through the soles of your feet. Even the water in the aquarium is shaking.

"We need to leave," Jerry says.

"No. We need to secure the animals." The sound grows louder.

"We can't do that if we're dead!" He pulls out his pepper spray. "Hope this does the trick. Hit 'em with a blast when they come through the door."

You glance down at your own spray. Whatever it is, it's about to burst through the door.

Use the pepper spray *ON PAGE 45*

To flee, *RUN BACK TO PAGE 22*

To stand your ground and wait, *GO TO PAGE 61*

44

"We came here to do a job," you say, feeling determined. "We got this far, I'm not turning around just because some stupid bird stole the code."

Jerry looks like he wants to argue, but he decides that's a useless effort. "Fine. I'll cover you from down here."

The scaffolding is made up of three platforms connected by individual ladders. The entire thing shifts as you step onto the rung of the first ladder. Swallowing your fear, you keep going.

You take it slowly, one rung at a time, never looking down. After fifteen feet the ladder ends and you step onto the first platform. The next ladder is much of the same.

As you reach the second platform a strong wind howls through the woods. The wooden scaffolding sways back and forth like a tree, creaking loudly with a thousand different joints.

Gripping the ladder, you look up. The final platform is just ten more feet above, with the open window. Through the glass you can see the metal rafters with the dozens of birds perched inside.

The wind dies down for a moment, and your ears perk up. What is that sound? It's coming from the window above, and it sounds like... like *growling.* Like an animal. But birds don't growl. Is it just a trick of the wind?

"You okay up there?" Jerry calls.

It's definitely growling, low and throaty like a cat. The scaffolding sways some more as the wind picks up. The final ladder doesn't seem so safe anymore.

To play it safe, *TURN BACK TO PAGE 40*
To climb higher, *GO TO PAGE 103*

45

There's no time, and you can't take any chances. You rip the pepper spray from your belt and hold it out in front of you, aimed at the broken doorway. The rumble is nearly there.

At the first sign of movement Jerry unloads a spray. Your own cannister hisses as a stream of irritating liquid covers everything before you.

After a long moment you lower it to see what you've struck. Your jaw drops.

A dozen black-and-white shapes stand in front of you, no taller than your waist. You realize why the building is so cold. "Penguins," you say. "Just penguins!"

"Ohh," Jerry says.

But it's too late, and you've already done the damage. The penguins begin squawking and flapping their arms, alarmed and confused. They begin running in circles around you, a violent pattering of webbed feet.

You just pepper sprayed some harmless penguins.

"The Captain told us not to harm any of the animals," you say.

"Dude, it was self defense!" Jerry says.

"Against *penguins?*"

"We didn't know!"

Jerry continues to argue, but you know that this is going to be a PR nightmare. No matter what order you restore to the zoo, you'll forever be known as the Corporal who sprayed a group of penguins. They certainly don't promote those kinds of officers to Sergeant. You did your best, but because of your itchy finger this is...

THE END

46

The sound of their legs skittering across the ground is too much for you. Knowing it is a mistake, you pull the pepper spray free from your belt and let loose a stream of toxic liquid at the first one on the right.

"Take that you eight-legged monster!" you yell. The first spider unleashes a scream like a tea kettle and jumps backwards.

You move the spray to the next spider. Jerry is yelling, but you can't tell what he's saying. You start to sidestep as you sense the other spiders to your right closing in, but your foot catches on some of the glass and you fall sideways. You throw your hand up to stop your fall, but that only scrapes glass across your palm.

The pepper spray goes flying.

"Jerry!" you yell, seeing the two remaining spiders closing in. From this angle you can see every hair on their long legs, the liquid dripping from their fangs. "Jerry!"

Discover your fate *ON PAGE 167*

47

The screen to the Power Station keycode glows red, taunting you. Do you know the code, or will you have to look around somewhere else?

To enter code 1-3-2, *GO TO PAGE 132*
To explore the Bird Bastion, *GO TO PAGE 67*
To check out the Food Forest, *GO TO PAGE 55*
To examine to Monkey Manor, *HEAD TO PAGE 51*

48

"Oh thank goodness," Jerry says, exhaling. "It's just a hippo."

The hippopotamus looms over you.

"Jerry," you whisper, "this is bad. This is *very* bad."

"Why? I was expecting a crocodile or something."

You take a step back. "Jerry. Hippos are literally the most dangerous animal in Africa. More people are killed by charging hippos than lions!"

Jerry pauses. "That can't be right."

"*Jerry!*"

The hippo moans, a low sound like a tuba. Jerry gets the picture and begins backing away with you. Then, without warning, he turns and begins swimming, splashing loudly while waving his arms and legs. This agitates the hippo, and it begins to move forward.

You turn and dive into the water, stretching forward to swim in long strokes.

It's almost like riding a wave, with the huge animal behind you, pushing the water forward. You reach the bank of the lake within seconds, and quickly jump onto land.

A look over your shoulder proves that the hippo has made it onto land and is still charging.

Jerry is three steps ahead of you, veering to the left. "Jerry, this way!" you yell, seeing a structure up ahead. "Jerry!"

He doesn't hear you. And he's slowly veering farther away.

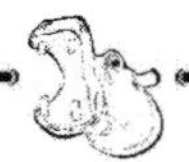

To follow Jerry, *VEER OVER TO PAGE 36*
To continue straight ahead, *RUN TO PAGE 50*

50

The Hippo is just too close; if you veer to the left to follow your partner then it will cut you off and trample you. It would be like a Golden Retriever running over an ant.

Your breath comes ragged as you squelch across the open field. The rain is falling harder now, enough that your clothes would be soaked–if they weren't already, you know, soaked. You hear the distant boom of thunder. Once, twice. Again and again.

That's when you realize it's not thunder, but the hippo's footsteps. It's still following you!

The building is still at least a hundred feet away. You're not sure if you'll make it. There's a lone tree up ahead with some low branches, within arm's reach. You're going to run right past it. You could probably swing up into safety. Though if you miss, or your hand slips...

The stomping is right behind you.

To continue toward the building, *GO TO PAGE 52*
To jump into the tree, *CLIMB TO PAGE 94*

51

You follow the path away from the Power Station and toward the Monkey Manor. Everything seems really peaceful on this side of the zoo, as if it has remained untouched from whatever chaos has befallen the rest.

The smell of the Monkey Manor hits you long before you see the structure. It actually does look like a mansion: it's shaped like a four story house, with open windows and doors and a porch around the front. The windows have bars, though, and as you draw closer you can see that the entire thing is just a wooden facade for a massive cage behind. The porch has a wire mesh to keep the monkeys inside.

"It looks so real from a distance," Jerry says. "Especially in the dark."

"Yeah." There's a sign next to the path. "It says here there are 216 monkeys in the zoo."

"216? That's a lot..."

The animals must have heard you talking, because they begin hooting and grunting. Soon the entire Monkey Manor is awake, animals swinging from one window to the other.

"It looks like none of them have escaped," you say. "They're still contained inside."

"Good. Then they can't bother us. Let's go find the employee office and see if we can–"

SPLAT.

Something wet lands on the ground next to you, like a water balloon. Except it's dark like mud, and gives off a terrible smell.

"Is that..." Jerry mutters.

SPLAT. Another large ball of feces lands on the other side of you.

"Uh huh," you say. "They can't bother us, huh?"

Soon all of the monkeys have climbed onto the porch and are hurling excrement at you.

To go back to the Power Station, *RUN TO PAGE 42*
To ignore the monkeys, *CONTINUE TO PAGE 57*
If you have the BANANAS, *TURN TO PAGE 81*

52

You near the tree and continue on past it, sprinting wildly, out of control. After a few seconds you're not sure if that was a mistake or not.

"Awwrrooooo," the hippo roars. It's so loud! And so *close.*

It quickly becomes apparent that you aren't going to make it. The building is just too far, and in a few seconds the hippo is going to trample you. You're going to need to bust out a duck-and-roll move. You haven't practiced that move since the Academy, but hey, it should be mostly muscle memory, right?

Roll a die (or pick a number at random):

If you rolled a 1 or 6, *DUCK TO PAGE 32*
If you rolled a 2, 3, 4, or 5, *ROLL TO PAGE 23*

53

"What's wrong, Jerry," you tease. "Afraid of a little animal? It's probably something harmless, like a koala."

You're afraid too, but Jerry doesn't need to know that. He stands up straight. "Fine. Let's go."

You begin climbing the steps, pausing at the sign on the wall that has the scratch marks. "Pretty big claws to do that," Jerry says.

You shake your head. "I don't know. This almost looks like..."

"Like what?"

"Like it was caused by something else. Maybe a beak."

Jerry snorts. "When did you become a biologist?"

"I had a parakeet," you say defensively. "He used to make marks in the bottom of his cage with his beak."

"I still think it's claws," Jerry mutters.

You continue up the stairs and around the corner. They end at one giant room, which appears to span almost the entire length of the building. Glass enclosures cover the walls; some take up the entire wall to the ceiling, and others are no bigger than what you would put a household turtle in.

Your flashlight glances off something on the ground. Something shiny and reflective. Jerry gasps.

It's glass. Half of the enclosures have been shattered.

"I figured out what exhibit is up here," Jerry says. Something in his voice sounds troubling.

You look at where he's aiming his flashlight. A wall sign covered in fake spiderweb says: "ARACHNID AUDITORIUM."

Uh oh. See what happens by *TURNING TO PAGE 58*

54

The rain hasn't let up, and you're instantly soaked again. There's no sign of the hippo, but you don't want to stick around. There's a path into the woods to the right, at the edge of the clearing. You sprint toward it.

When you're a safe distance away Jerry stops and puts his hands on his knees, panting. "Oh. Dude. I..."

"Don't call me dude."

He holds up a hand. "You don't know what I've been through. I ran from the hippo, but I guess you led it away. I thought I was in the clear until a pack of giraffes came running through! They were spooked by something in the woods. Nearly trampled me."

You chuckle. "Giraffes? You got scared by giraffes?"

"Hey!" he says, offended. "They're scary when they're in a group. I'm lucky. You just had the hippo to worry about. How'd you get away from it, anyways?"

You grin and say, "Tell you about it later. Let's go get those tranquilizer rifles, once and for all."

Head to the Warden Hut *ON PAGE 65*

55

You backtrack away from the Power Station and follow the path toward the Food Forest. It's a food court area, with an indoor restaurant and outdoor seating covered by a long awning.

Inside the restaurant everything has been ransacked. Tables and chairs knocked over. Napkins blowing across the ground. A gallon-sized bottle of ketchup has broken open on the floor, being pecked at by three exotic looking birds. There's also a cardboard box with a stack of Greensboro Gryphons baseball caps inside. That's a strange thing to see, but it's nowhere near the strangest thing in the room.

Taking a wide berth around the birds–they look mean!–you enter the kitchen. It's just as bad, with the added chaos of cookware and utensils strewn across the ground.

"I'd hate to be the cleaning crew tomorrow morning," you mutter.

"No kidding." Jerry looks around. "So what are we looking for?"

"I don't know. Anything useful. We need to get into the Power Station."

Jerry points. "Which do you want to check first? The Pantry, or the Freezer?"

Check the Freezer *ON PAGE 29*

Investigate the Pantry *ON PAGE 34*

56

You grip the heavy stone in your hand, taking a few breaths to harden your courage. The booming sound of the animal's footsteps is like something out of Jurassic Park.

"On the count of three," you whisper. "One. Two."

"Three!"

You lean out from under the tree and heave the stone into the woods behind you. Not waiting to see what happened, you turn and sprint in the direction of the Warden's Hut.

It gives you a ten second head start. Between the heavy raindrops and the sound of your breathing you can't even hear the beast. For a few, precious moments you begin to think you'll escape.

"Rodriguez, look out!"

Jerry's warning forces you to duck. It's just in the nick of time. A paw with three ferocious claws cuts through the air above you, right where your head just was.

The beast shrieks in anger.

You run faster, zig-zagging along the path. Jerry is yelling behind you, but he's following, so he must be okay. All you two can do is keep running and hope you make it.

The path rounds a corner and a chain link fence appears. Hoping it's not locked, you sprint at the gate and throw your shoulder against it.

It flies open.

As soon as Jerry's through you close the gate and find the latch. You wait for the beast to appear but nothing happens.

"It must have stopped chasing us," Jerry says.

"Yeah. Did you get a good look at that thing? It had paws, like a cat."

Jerry frowns. "I don't think so. I'm certain it had feathers."

You shrug it off. It was dark, and you were both terrified. You turn around and smile. "Here's the Warden Hut."

Approach the Warden Hut *ON PAGE 65*

57

"We need to get into that employee office," you decide. "Pinch your nose and let's keep going."

Jerry looks like he wants to make a joke about smell, but he keeps his mouth shut.

You circle wide around the Monkey Manor to look for the employee office. All the while the apes are bouncing up and down, tossing more and more malodorous muck in your direction.

"There's the door." Jerry points. "Employees only. And right next to the porch."

He's right. The door is only a few feet from the wire meshing of the porch. Approaching is not an enticing prospect.

But you need to get inside.

"So... what do we do?" Jerry asks.

At the path intersection is a waist-high podium. Its screen glows green.

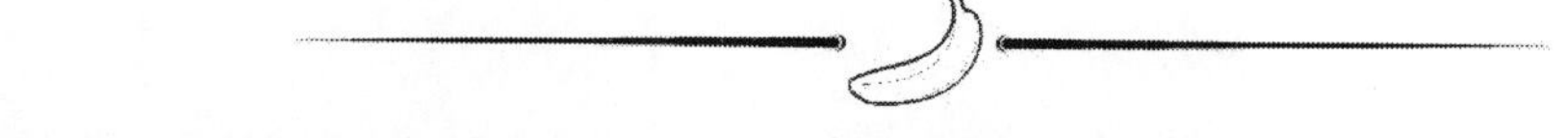

To try making a run for the door, *SPRINT TO PAGE 74*

To head back to the Power Station, *GO TO PAGE 42*

To check out the podium, *TURN TO PAGE 64*

58

The bird is moving impossibly fast. Just before it reaches you, right as it extends its talons, you throw yourself onto the disgusting floor.

The air behind rushes over you quickly, and for a moment you feel victorious. You glance up and see a brown hawk flying away from you. It flaps up toward the ceiling, circles twice, and then prepares to dive again.

You scramble up, suppressing a gag as your hand digs through a layer of bird droppings. "It's coming back!" you yell to Jerry, who is standing there, dumbfounded. "Jerry, keep going!"

You run for the door. But you hesitated too long, gave the hawk too much time. It's diving fast, and it's about to reach you. You're going to have to jump again.

FLIP A COIN!

If it lands heads, *JUMP TO PAGE 37*
If it lands tails, *DIVE TO PAGE 131*

59

There's glass everywhere, covering every bit of floor. As you look closer you can now see that all of the class displays on the left side of the room are broken.

"We'd better hurry then," you say, jogging across the room.

Glass crunches beneath your boots as you head toward the zoo employee office, a door on the right. All of the glass cages here are unbroken, and soon the floor becomes clean to walk on. There's a long gash in the wall, but you ignore it to get inside the office. The door opens easily.

There's a single desk with papers and a powerless computer. An official looking note is taped to the screen:

ZOO ANNOUNCEMENT

Attention Emma's team: I'm not joking when I say that Project Fusion needs bigger claws. Bigger! Kids want to see something scary, not something barely more dangerous than a housecat.

-Warden Oxford

There are more notes on the desk, but you glance over them. Feeling safer, you hand the note to Jerry and wander back into the main room, stopping in front of the wall outside the office. The gash is ten feet long and has broken through the drywall, showing the support beams behind. What could have caused that? "I know that zoo announcement says claws," you call to Jerry, "but I swear this looks like a beak."

"Hey, stop crunching around on the glass out there," Jerry responds. "Some of those shards are several inches long."

You glance down at your feet. "*Dude*," you say, "I'm not moving."

"Well then..."

You freeze. You hear it too, the distinct sound of weight being pressed on broken glass.

Turn around *ON PAGE 60*

60

You spin, afraid of what you'll see.

It's immediately obvious what's causing the noise. Four bulbous objects move across the dark floor. The cone of your flashlight hits them.

Spiders. Four of them, like lightbulbs the size of German Shepherds.

"Oh crap!" you yell. "Jerry..."

"Uhh..." he mutters. You think he's standing in the doorway, but you're too afraid to pull your eyes away from the arachnids as they move closer. "Just a second!"

"Jerry! What are you doing!" The spiders are only ten feet away.

"Don't move! I have a way I can distract them!"

You take a step back but feel the wall behind you. The spiders have spread out, like wolves on the hunt. "Jerry!"

"Don't move!"

Your hand brushes against your pepper spray. You could probably get one or two, but all four?

To pepper spray the spiders, *JUMP TO PAGE 46*
To listen to Jerry, wait *OVER ON PAGE 72*
If you'd rather run away, *FLEE TO PAGE 99*

61

"We're here to help, not harm," you insist. "Put your spray down and see what it is first."

"But Rodriguez..."

"Do it!"

He lowers his spray but keeps it in his hands. After a moment you retrieve yours and do the same. Just in case.

The rumbling becomes a roar. There's movement at the door, and then a herd of animals pours through. They're no taller than your waist, with white on their bellies and black everywhere else. "Penguins!" you say with a laugh as the stampede enters the room. They don't even slow as they rush past you and down the hall. Even Jerry laughs.

They disappear through another doorway, though thankfully still in the building. "They're contained as long as they stay inside," you say. "So we don't need to do anything more. Let's go check out that office they came out of."

Even Jerry laughs. "Fine by me, Corporal."

Check out the employee office *ON PAGE 62*

62

There's a small changing room with lockers. Everything smells nasty, like fish. "Nobody tells you that penguins stink," Jerry says.

"They don't stink under water," you say.

"Well no, because..." he trails off as he gets it. "Haha. Making jokes, huh dude?"

You open a locker and glance inside. There's a Greensboro Gryphons cap but not much else. "Don't call me dude," you mutter as you grab a piece of paper. It's another message from the warden, printed on official lettering.

ZOO ANNOUNCEMENT.

All Penguin Palace feeding rations are to be cut by 10% until further notice. Another project at the zoo has taken priority, and we're nearly out of our supply of fish. Don't like it? Complain to the supply chief.

-Warden Oxford

"Another project," Jerry reads, leaning over your shoulder. "Do you think that means..."

"Yeah," you say. Project Fusion seems to be affecting everything around here. "Will you make yourself useful, Jerry?"

He flashes a toothy grin and holds up a small card. "Found this in the other locker. It seems most of the buildings have a code needed to get inside."

You take it and squint at it by the light of your flashlight:

WARDEN HUT CODE: 122

You smile right back at him. "You're not so useless after all!"

You slip in into your pocket so you won't forget.

"Okay. Let's head outside. This building is secure."

Continue *ON PAGE 21*

63

You nod to Jerry, an unspoken signal among long-time partners. Both of you count to three in your heads.

POP POP.

Two darts whiz toward the hyenas. One yelps and lurches backwards, a pink dart sticking out from its fur. It teeters back and forth before curling up to go to sleep.

But the other dart missed.

"I don't know how I missed!" Jerry says, fumbling to reload his rifle. "I never miss!" His hands are shaking.

The remaining three hyenas look at their sleeping comrade with confusion. You have a moment to get away.

Hopefully.

Run away *TO PAGE 166*

64

You approach the podium. Because it still has power you assumed it was important, but as you approach you see a sign that says, "Trivia booth! Win a token to the Observation Tower!"

"Huh. I guess they put this on the emergency power circuit by mistake."

The screen has a single question flashing:

Red colobus monkeys of Zanzibar regularly eat what unusual item?

1. **Charcoal**
2. **Plastic**
3. **Aluminum**

"That's a weird question," Jerry says. "Do you know the answer?"

To guess **Charcoal,** *TURN TO PAGE 145*
To guess **Plastic,** *FLIP TO PAGE 157*
To guess **Aluminum,** *GO TO PAGE 162*

65

It's a nondescript cement building with a flat roof, sort of like a bunker. There's a larger door on the side to a garage of some kind. The entire structure looks like it could withstand a bomb blast. Everything is dark since the lights in the park haven't been turned back on yet.

You approach the main door. It's metal and electronic, far more elaborate than something you'd expect to find at a zoo. "There's a keycode entry," you say. "It still has power, apparently. Must be on the emergency system."

Jerry takes a few steps around the side. "And there's a ladder over here leading to the roof."

If you have the code to the Warden Hut, *TURN TO THAT PAGE*
If not, climb the ladder to the roof *ON PAGE 24*

66

Jerry is standing in the corner, next to a vending machine. "Are you still complaining about being hungry?" you say. "Jerry, it's late. We have to focus and–"

You cut off as you come closer. Behind the vending machine is a small podium with a green screen. It glows, beckoning.

Jerry gives you a smug smile.

The screen says "Trivia booth! Win a token to the Observation Tower!" There's a single question listed:

Which species of bear is so dangerous that it's recommended you play dead when encountering it?

1. **Black Bear**
2. **Grizzly Bear.**

"Hey, I remember this," you say. "It was one of the factoids at the entrance to the park."

Jerry nods. "Okay, smarty-pants. What's the answer then?"

To select **Black Bear,** *TURN TO PAGE 163*
To choose **Grizzly Bear,** *GO TO PAGE 147*

67

You take the path around the side, away from the Power Station. You and Jerry remain silent as you follow the cone of your flashlights.

A giant glass dome rises up in front of you. It's *enormous*, at least ten stories tall. It's made of hundreds of geometric pieces, like a humongous glass soccer ball. There's some wooden scaffolding on the right side, with buckets and squeegees. They must be cleaning the glass.

There only appears to be one entrance. Everything is quiet as you approach the door. A keycode glows next to it. "You need keycodes to get everywhere," you mutter.

If you know the code, *GO TO THAT PAGE*
If not, head back to the Power Station *ON PAGE 47*

68

You each grab one side of the tray of steak and turn around. Two of the lions have already entered the room, heads hanging low, steps slow and careful. The lead lion's mouth is open is a wicked snarl.

The plastic tray clatters as you drop it on the floor in front of you. The lions flinch back, but quickly resume their approach.

"Please work," Jerry mutters. "Please!"

You both grab a handful of fillets. The lions are blocking the door, so you need to be smart about this. If you can get them closer you can slip around the other side of the table and behind them.

Aiming carefully, you toss the first steak in front of the tray. You throw down another one, a little bit farther. Jerry gets the idea and does the same. You repeat the process four more times until there's a line of juicy steaks leading right to the tray.

Then you wait.

The first lion sniffs the steak and quickly scoops it into its mouth, swallowing it in one gulp. It must be the alpha because it turns and growls at the others, then approaches the next steak and eats that too.

The others draw closer, on either side of the alpha. They don't even care about you anymore. They're too focused on the real meat. They begin to fight over the next steak, and then the one after that, rolling and growling.

While they're occupied, you slip around the other side of the table as quietly and calmly as you can. By then they've pounced on the full tray of meat, throwing it to the side and tossing steaks around like toys. You reach the door and all calmness disappears. You and Jerry run out into the storm.

Try to find safety *ON PAGE 54*

69

You nod to Jerry, an unspoken signal among long-time partners. Both of you count to three in your heads.

POP POP.

Two darts whiz toward the hyenas. Inexplicably, both miss, tumbling through the trees behind.

Jerry stares, dumbfounded.

"I thought you were a good shot!" you say, not even bothering to load another dart.

"I am! I don't know how I missed!" He looks up at the dark lantern above you. "Maybe if we had turned the power back on first..."

You've missed your chance, and the hyenas quickly surround you. You realize there's more important things than just getting some firepower. That's going to be a tough lesson to remember though, because as the hyenas advance you're painfully aware this is...

THE END

70

The office is the cleanest one you've seen in the entire park, with precise stacks of papers and a computer screen that looks like it gets dusted often. A Greensboro Gryphon cap rests on top of the cabinets. You check the drawers of the desk but there's no Tower Tokens inside, just various snake paraphernalia and other employee tools.

There's a note pinned to a bulletin board that catches your attention:

ZOO ANNOUNCEMENT.

After the incident with Marlene, Project Fusion is hereby closed to all personnel except myself. All feeding will be administered by me, under the strictest of security settings. And don't worry about Marlene–the hospital says the claw marks were not very deep and she is expected to make a full recovery. Please sign the 'Get Well' card for her in my office.

-Warden Oxford

"Are we sure we even want to get a Tower Token now?" Jerry asks. "Claw marks don't sound appealing. I think I'd like to keep my distance."

"I'd like to get one anyways, just to be safe," you say. "But it doesn't look like there's anything in here. I guess we'll just head back to the tower."

Jerry clears his throat. "There's a trivia podium in the lobby."

What? *TURN TO PAGE 107*

71

You look out the window of the closed door in time to see the hippo slowing to a stop. It takes one long look at the building and turns around, stomping away almost as fast as it had arrived.

Whew!

Unfortunately, there's still no sign of Jerry.

Fortunately, you have your radio. And it's water-proof.

"Officer Holman, come in. Officer Holman, this is Officer Rodriguez. Come in."

Silence.

Well, maybe his radio is malfunctioning. Or he dropped it. You press down the receiver anyways, just in case. "Jerry, I've taken shelter in a building at the end of the field, from where we were running." You turn and look around. "It's like a barn, with green paint on the outside. It's open to the elements on one side, with some hay strewn around a cement floor. It's dark, so I think we're safe here, at least..."

"Dude!"

The sound sends you jumping backward, even though you know it's Jerry. "You scared me!"

He smiles white teeth. "Sorry, I meant to be quieter... but I was excited to see you! You'll never believe what I just..."

He trails off as a scratching sound comes from inside the building.

Your fingers brush against your belt. There's nothing there. The pepper spray is gone! It must have fallen off earlier.

You both look back and forth, scanning the darkness, searching for movement or the source of the sound.

There, to the right. Hidden in the shadows, you think you saw something. You both stand there, focusing on that area. Waiting.

A pair of glowing yellow eyes open. *Uh oh,* you think. *Time to get out of here.*

A second pair of eyes open to your left. Then a third to the right. Whatever they are, there's a lot of them. And they have you two surrounded.

To find out what they are, *TURN TO PAGE 114*

If you're too scared to continue, *CLOSE THE BOOK AND GO PLAY OUTSIDE INSTEAD.*

72

Years of working together has created an intense bond of trust between you and Officer Jerry Holman. "I'm waiting," you say with a shaky voice, "but you'd better have a good plan!"

He responds with a loud clatter, throwing something around in the office.

The spiders draw closer, their legs thick and covered with black hair. They've spread out, as if they're hunting. And there's only one prey they appear to care about.

"Jerry..."

The spider directly in front of you crouches down as if it's going to leap. You pull out your pepper spray and prepare to use it.

A piercing sound cuts the air, like a dog whistle but more electronic. You clutch your ears and fall to your knees. It feels like someone is drilling into your ears!

Through clenched eyes you notice the four spiders are trembling. One of them takes a step back, teetering as if dizzy. Another follows in the same condition. They stumble that way across the room and into one of the broken glass enclosures.

The sound cuts out and Jerry appears next to you. He lowers a hand. "Come on, get up."

Get up *ON PAGE 101*

73

The lion enclosure is sort of like a barn, with a concrete floor and hay strewn all around. One large door is open on the other side, allowing a hissing wind to run through. There's an office on the left.

You step into the office and see a mess of folders on the desk. A Greensboro Gryphons cap hangs from a peg on the wall. In the corner is an open fridge, where Jerry must have gotten the steaks.

Grabbing the first paper you see on the desk, you realize it's another message from the Warden:

ZOO ANNOUNCEMENT.

Dave, we're going to need more lion DNA for... another project. I don't want any more practical jokes of yours, just give us what we need. And fast!

-Warden Oxford

You show the announcement to Jerry. "I told you there was something to their shaved legs!"

"I still don't understand why they would need lion DNA." He shakes his head. "Whatever this Project Fusion is, I'm beginning to suspect it's the reason everything has gone haywire at this place."

"Jerry, that's the first sensible thing you've said all day."

He puts a hand on his chest in mock pain. "You insult me, Rodriguez." He pulls a card out of his pocket. "After all, wouldn't you say it's awfully useful to have one of these?"

It's a plain rectangle of plastic, like a credit card. Indented into it are the words:

WARDEN HUT CODE: 122

"I take back everything I've ever said about you," you say. "And you did save me from those lions. Okay. I should have listened to you when we first got here. Let's go get those tranquilizer rifles."

Head to the Warden Hut *ON PAGE 65*

74

"On the count of three we run for the door," you say. It's only a hundred feet or so.

"What if it's locked?"

"We'll worry about that when we get there." You take a deep breath. "One. Two..."

"Three!"

You sprint forward. The monkeys go nuts, jumping up and down and shrieking with excitement. Balls of dung begin landing all around you. It's like a World War One military bombardment. Except, you know. With poop.

One glob hits you on the knee. Jerry must have been hit too because he cries out, disgusted. The smell is growing worse as you near. You're almost there!

It's tough to see in the darkness, and your foot slips on something foul. Your legs fly out from under you and the ground slams into your back.

"Ughhh," you groan.

Jerry appears over you. "Come on! You can't stay here!" He grabs your hand and pulls you up right as a ball of filth hits the side of his head. "Eww..."

You run the rest of the way, throwing yourself against the wall. The door opens. You slip inside and slam it behind you.

"That was fun," you say sarcastically. Your uniform is coated in brown.

Abruptly, a speaker in the ceiling crackles to life. *"Animal smell detected. Breach assumed. Initiating lockdown."*

The door makes a strange clicking sound.

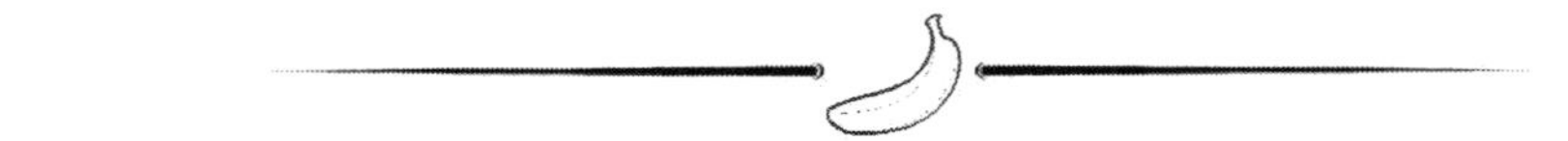

What just happened? *GO TO PAGE 76*

The path winds through the woods. A soft patter fills the air as it begins to rain, though you are mostly covered by the trees. You reach a fork in the road. Straight ahead is the Warden Hut, and to the right is the Safari Zone.

"Glad you're not leading us around in circles," Jerry says.

Before you can tease him back, there's a booming noise ahead. Both of you freeze, tensing. The only sound is the patter of the rain all around you.

"What was that?" Jerry whispers.

"It sounded like a truck," you respond. It was huge. That couldn't have been anything other than heavy machinery.

Another boom, this time close enough to feel in your feet. You take a step back when a screech cuts the air.

AHHCAWWWWWW!

It's a combination between a siren and a shriek, like nothing you've ever heard. It came from directly ahead of you, in the direction of the Warden Hut.

And it's coming closer.

"Look," Jerry stammers, "I don't think we should be out here. I don't like being out in the rain. You can catch a chill. My wife always says..."

He's mumbling, terrified. You grab his arm. "We need those tranquilizer darts."

He whips his head back and forth. "You still want to go forward? Past *that?*"

"Why not? I bet if we sprint we can make it to the Warden Hut in time."

You think of what Captain Beckett told you. If you take care of this, the promotion is as good as yours. But the path to the Warden Hut will surely take you right past the beast...

To take a chance for the Warden Hut, *GO TO PAGE 102*

To go around to the other path, *SLIDE TO PAGE 30*

76

Jerry jiggles the door handle. "It's locked!"

"How is that possible?"

"Lockdown complete," the speaker hisses. *"Animals contained."*

"We're not animals!"

You say, "We sure smell like them."

"How could they have a system like this?" Jerry tries the door handle again. "Oh, come on!"

You search around the office but it's no use. The security system appears to be on the backup power grid, and with the normal power still out the computer in the office won't turn on. You find the keycode to get into the Bird Bastion but by then it just doesn't matter.

You're falling asleep when the door suddenly opens. A large man wearing a biohazard suit stands in the doorway. The side of his suit says, "Animal Control" on it.

"What is that *smell*?" he says through his mask. He sounds like Darth Vader.

You've been in the park all night and accomplished almost nothing. Worse, you're covered in filth when you meet Captain Beckett at the park entrance. He's so furious with you that he promises to tell the entire police station that they found you locked in a room covered in animal excrement. You'll never live it down.

And that promotion is as good as gone. Maybe you'll find a way to earn it in the future, but it'll be a long time before Captain Beckett forgives you. And so you have reached...

THE END

77

The office is rather plain, with two desks and computer terminals and stacks of papers all around. There's a dry erase board on one wall with animal feeding schedules written in red, green, and blue marker.

One piece of paper on the desk looks more official than the others, so you pick it up. "Hey, this is from the Warden," you say.

ZOO ANNOUNCEMENT

Unfortunately, due to competing demands, all research on the zoo's Gorilla Spider project must cease immediately. If you have any further questions please contact me directly. And as a reminder: discussing such projects with other zoo employees is STRICTLY FORBIDDEN. This rule will be enforced by termination, if necessary.

-Warden Oxford

"Gorilla Spider?" Jerry shakes his head. "See what I mean about the tranq rifles?"

You nod. "Yeah, yeah. You were right."

Jerry leans back. "Hold on, let me get my phone out. I want to record you saying that, for evidence."

"Shut up." You push around some other items on the desk. "Hey, look at this." It's a small card with a single sentence imprinted into the face:

BEAR ABODE CODE: 135

"Bear Abode," you say. "I'm not sure I like the sound of that."

"So you *are* afraid of something?" Jerry asks. "Well at least I've made one discovery tonight."

You exit the office and see the red EXIT sign ahead. It leads to another winding path through the woods.

Follow the path *ON PAGE 11*

78

A line of black, windowless vans comes roaring around the corner. One at a time they halt in front of you in the clearing by the Visitor's Center. You and Jerry share a look.

"Duuude," he says.

You begin to tell him not to call you that when the door to the first van opens. You immediately recognize the two bars on the man's uniform. Indicating the rank of Captain.

You scramble forward and salute. "Captain Beckett, sir!"

Jerry is still standing there, holding the tranquilizer rifle. Only when you clear your throat does he jump next to you and mimic the salute.

Captain Beckett eyes the two of you. He's a bull of a man, sixty years old with broad shoulders and muscular arms. His uniform is tight and orderly, his face chiseled with discipline.

"Sir," you begin, "a status update. We have–"

He silences you with a hand and stares past you. "Corporal," he says quietly, "you didn't *kill* that animal, did you?"

79

You turn around and see the zebra on the ground some distance away. You look back at the Captain and smile. "Of course not, sir. He's sedated. When we arrived at the zoo we followed Warden Oxford's instructions from an email: we restored power to the park and then retrieved the tranquilizer darts. We were driving around sedating as many animals as we could when you arrived."

Another man hops out of the passenger side of the first van. He looks like Teddy Roosevelt come alive: tan safari uniform, round spectacles, and reddish mustache. He looks around at the animals on the ground and beams.

"Well done! Absolutely well done. I'm glad *someone* listened to orders. Dave ran scared at the first sign of trouble." He turns to the Captain. "You sent two fine officers, Beckett."

Captain Beckett gives a hint of a smile. "I suppose I did."

"Tell me," Oxford continues, "did you happen to see anything... *unusual* while you were here?"

"You mean Project Fusion?" Jerry blurts.

Oxford leans back. "I'm not sure you are supposed to know what that is, officer... Holman." He squints at the name tag. "And how did you come by this information?"

"It was mentioned on a bunch of your Zoo Announcements," you interject. "And as a matter of fact, we did come across it. It tore apart the Bird Bastion and knocked a bunch of trees down."

"What is it?" Jerry asks. "Officer Rodriguez and I have been debating it the entire night. She thinks it has paws like a cat, but I'm positive it has a beak, like a bird. Plus, it can fly."

This seems to make Warden Oxford very uncomfortable. He looks at the two of you for a long while, as if deciding what to tell you.

80

"And where did you last see Project Fusion?" Warden Oxford finally asks.

"It flew to the top of the Observation Tower," you say. "We were going to pursue it but the Zoo Announcement in the jeep said it was dangerous and should be avoided.

"Unfortunately the nature of the animal is classified," he finally says. He pulls out a radio and says, "Bring in the birds. It's on the Observation Tower again."

Jerry looks like he's about to argue some more, but then a steady *THUMP-THUMP THUMP* cuts the air. Moments later two military-style helicopters burst into view, shooting over you and flying deeper into the park. You turn around with everyone else and watch them split apart, coming around the top of the Observation Tower in a pincer maneuver.

The beast shrieks, long and wrathful.

"It would have been especially impressive if you had brought that beast to heel," Oxford sighs. "But oh well. You did marvelous anyways." And with that Oxford climbs back in the van and drives away, disappearing down the road leading to the Observation Tower.

Captain Beckett looks at you and Officer Holman as if not sure what to make of the whole thing.

"You heard him, sir," you say. "We did *marvelous*. I think we deserve some rest and relaxation... and maybe a promotion, as well?"

"He also said it would have been more impressive if you'd brought down that thing. We'll talk about this in the morning. Report to the station at 08:00." He gives you one final look of appraisal and strides away.

"Well. We're alive, huh?" Jerry says as the two of you head back to the police car. "Better than I expected, all things considered."

"Yeah, I suppose so." The sound of the Project Fusion beast–whatever it is–disturbs the night again. Oh, it would have been impressive to take it down! But you've ended up on top and done your best, which you've reached a satisfying version of...

THE END

81

It seems obvious once you realize it. "Jerry, give me those bananas."

He looks hurt. "No! I was going to eat them."

"I paid for them."

"Yeah, but..."

"JERRY, hand them over."

Sighing, Jerry pulls the bananas from his pocket and thrusts them in your direction. You take them and return your gaze to the building.

The monkeys must have realized what you have. A hushed silence falls over them as they stare at you. Their dark eyes glow in the moonlight as they await your move.

You walk toward the Employees Only door on the side of the Monkey Manor. They follow along behind the wire mesh of the porch, watching quietly. None of them are throwing anything anymore. You hold out one of the bananas in front of you so they can see it. The entire thing feels like a hostage exchange.

Right before reaching the door, you toss the banana through a hole in the mesh. The apes pounce on it.

Jerry has already opened the door to the employee office. You follow inside and close it behind. That wasn't so hard.

Investigate the office *ON PAGE 16*

82

You sit in the tree for a few minutes, periodically attempting to hail Jerry on the radio. There's no sound other than your own voice and the patter of rain on the leaves.

"Jerry, you're making me awfully lonely. And worried. I'd feel a lot better if you showed up again."

"Officer Holman, come in. If you've broken a leg I'm *not* helping to drag you home. You can just limp, no matter how many hippos chase us."

"Jerry, your birthday is next month, and I'm not getting you anything. Not if you don't stop screwing around. Jerry!"

Eventually you give up. Either Jerry's lost his radio or something worse has happened. You try not to think about the latter.

The hippo has been gone for a while. It's probably safe. The rain has even begun to let up, at least as best as you can tell from up in the tree.

Something to the right catches your eye. At first you thought it was the moon, but it's much lower than that. It's a shiny sphere floating in the air! What on earth could that be? It's like an enormous firefly.

Could this be Project Fusion? Mutant fireflies?

It comes close, drifting through the branches. It's nearly within reach. You extend your hand...

83

Your fingers float through the air toward the shiny, round orb. It's nearly there.

You try touching the object, but something stops you. And the orb abruptly disappears! "What the..."

The orb reappears and there's an incredibly loud noise:

HOOOOOOONK.

It's like a huge kazoo, ridiculously loud. And it startles you so much that you jerk backwards and slip from the branch. "Ahhh!"

You hit a few branches on the way down, fingers scrambling around for purchase. There's none to be had and you slam into the ground. The force knocks the wind from you.

Groaning in the mud, you turn to look up from where you just came. That's when you realize the orb was actually the eyeball of an animal. A very *tall* animal.

A giraffe!

It lowers its neck to inspect you, the shiny orb coming close to your face. It doesn't seem to know what to make of you. Then it raises straight up and gallops off on long, stilt-like legs.

Chuckling to yourself, you push up to your knees. Now you're glad Jerry is nowhere to be found, because if he saw that you'd never hear the end of it.

Once you catch your breath you lean down into the radio on your shoulder. "Alright Jerry, I'm going to head back to the Warden Hut. Something embarrassing just happened and you missed it, so I hope you're not just playing hide and seek." You give a little laugh. It's funny, in a cartoonish sort of way.

Until you hear a growl behind you.

Uh oh. Turn around *ON PAGE 108*

84

You take the steps on anxious feet. From here the walls of the stairwell block your view of the beast, so you have no idea what it's doing. Hopefully Jerry will tranquilize it if it does anything dangerous.

Hopefully.

You're near the top of the stairs when your head clears the roof. You raise it slowly, peering out over the flat area.

The animal is near the edge to the left, about ten feet away. It's still just a dark silhouette, but you can make out more distinct features: a thick body, four legs... and a long tail. The tail is the closest part to you, and it's nothing like a bird's. It has fur, like a cat.

Before you can do anything else, a voice calls out. "Hey? Hey! Who's there?"

It startles you so much that you fall backwards onto the other side of the stairs, landing on the flat roof. With a crackle of electricity all of the lights around the perimeter of the roof cut on, bathing the whole scene with white light. For a moment you're blinded, and when vision returns the animal looks over you like a giant.

It's head is unmistakably that of an eagle, with a yellow beak and white feathers behind intense eyes. And the spread wings are a bird's as well, though massive, at least twenty feet long. But the rest of the body doesn't make sense. The torso is covered with beige fur, with the muscular haunches of a cat. Its hind legs are also cat-like, with thick paws resting on the ground. And the tail you saw earlier.

86

"What..." you stammer, terrified. "What are you?"

The beast opens its beak and screams with fury. For a moment you know this is about to be the end.

Until a man steps up next to it, ducking under the wing. "It's a gryphon."

You're so shocked you don't know what question to ask first. "A what?"

The man with the zoo uniform pats the gryphon's chest. "Mythological creature. Half lion, half eagle. Beautiful, isn't she?" He points to the top of the stairs. "You triggered the motion sensors, which turn on all the lights. That's why we stayed away from it. You're lucky she only got spooked for a minute. If I weren't here..."

The gryphon cocks its head at you as if curious. It almost sounds like it's purring.

A voice down below reminds you that you're not alone. "Rodriguez? Rodriguez! Are you okay? What's going on?"

Wary of the huge gryphon, you get to your feet. "It's okay Jerry. Come on up. But do it slowly, so you don't scare it."

"Scare *what*?"

He's speechless as he climbs the stairs and sees the animal. While he gets used to it, you ask the zoo employee, "What's your name?"

"I'm Dave."

"We saw an email at the Visitor's Center," you say. "From the Warden. He wanted you to subdue Project Fusion."

Dave smiles. "Yeah. I told him I was leaving, but that was just to throw him off. The whole time I've been in here, trying to track down Gabrielle before she hurt herself."

87

Jerry swallows. "Gabrielle?"

"Yeah, that's what we call her." He sits cross-legged on the ground and the gryphon copies him, folding her wings and laying her head in his lap. She closes her eyes as Dave begins to rub behind her ear.

"Attendance hasn't been good at the zoo. So the scientists, under the supervision of Warden Oxford, began working on an exciting new animal exhibit. One that was sure to attract a lot more visitors. Something the kids have never seen."

"Project Fusion," you say with realization. "Fusion, because you're combining two animals."

"Exactly. And what better animal than the mascot of the Greensboro baseball team? It wouldn't be too hard, or so the scientists told us. Mankind has come a long way in the field of genetics. They tried some other combinations first. Hopefully you didn't come across the Gorilla Spiders over in the Insect Enclosure. Anyways, once they were confident enough they began trying to splice lion genes with those from an eagle. Within a year they had Gabrielle here."

The gryphon purrs louder at hearing her name.

"Well the science was the easy part. What they *couldn't* predict was that she would be so stubborn. Yeah, I called you stubborn, girl. Don't deny it."

"Stubborn?" Jerry asks. He's slowly growing more comfortable with the situation.

"Yeah. She *hates* being locked up. She's too big. Those wings are as long as a school bus, and made to fly. And I'm sure you can guess that they don't just let her fly in the open sky. Well I wasn't even working on her project, I was assigned to the Penguin Palace. But I discovered her one evening when I was the only one here in the park. I've been visiting her every night since then. Talking to her, feeding her treats. She likes the company."

88

You say, "So what went wrong with the park?"

"Nothing went *wrong*," Dave said. "It just... didn't go exactly as I had planned. I tried sabotaging the power, so the enclosures would open and Gabrielle would be free. But all that did was shock one of the other employees. So I waited until a night when I was alone, when the other night shift employee called in sick. That's when I went to the Power Station and disabled part of the backup functionality before blowing the main circuit. The backup generator came on, but it had no power to the Bird Bastion, which is where they let Gabrielle fly at night."

"You tried to set her free!"

"I tried, but like I said it didn't go smoothly. Instead of going through the open door at ground level, Gabrielle tried smashing through the glass dome! I had to climb up onto the scaffolding on the outside and smash it with a wrench to help her. But I didn't break open a large-enough hole, and when she flew out she cut her wing on the glass."

Gently laying her head down, Dave gets up and walks around behind her wing. You make a wide circle around the animal and join him. He sticks his hands into the puffs of feathers and parts them so you can see a long, deep gash.

He must have touched it, because Gabrielle swings her head around and hisses at him.

"Easy, girl. Just showing them what's wrong." He looks at you. "She can fly, but only for a few seconds at a time."

You share a look with Jerry, remembering your orders from Captain Beckett. "Dave, I know you care about Gabrielle, but she's a wild animal. And she's enormous! It's dangerous for her to be wild."

He shakes his head wildly. "No. No, she's not dangerous! She only eats fish, nothing else. She's shy, believe it or not. She just wants to be left alone. Honest."

Jerry is still holding his rifle like he's ready to use it. It's obvious what he thinks you should do. You look down at Gabrielle, staring into her eyes. She looks at you with the pitifulness of a cat at the animal shelter. Pleading with you.

This isn't some vicious animal, you realize. *She's a misunderstood creature that doesn't belong here.*

And you have the power to let her go.

89

"Jerry, do you still have that medical kit in your pocket?"

He fishes around on the outside of his uniform. "Sure. Right here."

You take it and open it up. Rolls of gauze, bandaging tape, and some needles filled with a liquid pain killer. "Let's bandage this girl up."

Dave shows you how to hold apart the feathers while he cuts off lengths of gauze. He gives her shot of the liquid painkillers. Gabrielle hisses through her tiny bird nostrils while he applies the bandages and tapes them into place. By the end of it Jerry has put down his rifle and is petting the gryphon on its neck, whispering soothing words to her. The moment is so peaceful you don't even tease him for it.

"That ought to do it," Dave says, wiping his hands. "Okay, Gabrielle. Give it a test."

The gryphon obeys, flexing her wing open and closed. She still doesn't seem 100% functional, but she's much better than before.

"Now what?" Jerry asks.

A noise down on the ground is your answer. The three of you rush to the roof railing and see a line of headlights snaking its way through the forest. In your direction.

Dave runs back to his animal. "Gabrielle, I know you're still in pain, but you have to go. They're coming!"

The bird–cat?–cocks her head at him, confused.

He points to the sky. "You have to *go*. It's time, like we talked about. The ocean is that way, with all the fish you could ever want."

The sound of car engines drew nearer.

The gryphon seems to understand now. She makes a sad sound and gently headbutts Dave, rubbing her head against his chest. Then, to your surprise, she does the same to you, purring all the while. Jerry comes last.

With a final look she leaps into the air, wings beating so strongly that it whips your hair and clothes around. Her wing beats are a little lopsided, but she steadily flies toward the ocean, in the opposite direction as the approaching cars.

90

The three of you run down the stairs, silently proud of your actions.

You reach the ground just as a line of black, windowless vans comes roaring around the corner and into the clearing. One by one they zoom past and halt at the base of the Observation Tower.

The door to the first van opens. You immediately recognize the two bars on the man's uniform. Indicating the rank of Captain.

You scramble forward and salute. "Captain Beckett, sir!"

Jerry is still standing there, looking surprised. Only when you clear your throat does he jump next to you and mimic the salute.

Captain Beckett eyes the two of you. He's a bull of a man, sixty years old with broad shoulders and muscular arms. His uniform is tight and orderly, his face chiseled with discipline. You can't tell if he's happy or angry.

Before he can say anything, another man hops out of the passenger side of the first van. He looks like Teddy Roosevelt come alive: tan safari uniform, round spectacles, and reddish mustache.

"What happened to it!" he exclaims with a formal, precise English accent. "My creature. It was on the roof of the Observation Tower not five minutes ago. What have you done?"

You clear your throat before answering. "Warden Oxford I presume? We have contained most of the zoo. Some of the animals are still on the loose, but we did the best with what we had. Per your instructions, we visited the Warden Hut and retrieved..."

"Forget my instructions." He waves a hand. "*Project Fusion.* My creature. What have you done with it?"

"*Her*," Dave says. "Not *it*."

The Warden rounds on him. "I've had enough out of you, Dave. I know you're behind this somehow. Now, good officers. Have you seen it?"

You put on a confused look. "Project Function, sir?"

"Project *Fusion*. The premiere research project at the zoo. Do not feign confusion. If you've been here all night then surely you saw it!"

"*Her*," mutters Dave. "Not *it*."

You shake your head. "I'm sorry, Warden, but we have no idea what you're talking about."

Jerry nods. "No idea at all."

91

The Warden looks at each of you one at a time, searching your faces for any hint of a lie. You get the impression he's a man who is good at reading people.

After an uncomfortable amount of time he grits his teeth and grabs Dave. "I want you to tell me everything that happened," he says, leading him away. "Everything!"

"Sir, I don't know anything. The power went out, and since then I've been hiding..." they trail off in the distance.

You and Jerry are left standing in front of Captain Beckett. He crosses arms and takes a deep breath. "So. Officers Rodriguez, Holman. What really happened?"

"It happened just like we said it did," you say carefully. "We secured as much of the zoo as we could, then retrieved the tranquilizer rifles from the Warden Hut to take down some of the bigger animals."

"Just like that," Jerry repeats.

"Sir, if you were expecting more, then I apologize. I take full responsibility for any failures in our mission tonight. Officer Holman and I did our best." You glance over in the direction of the Warden. "I suppose that was not good enough."

Captain Beckett arches an eyebrow. "Rodriguez, I've played poker with you. And you have a terrible poker face."

You blush.

"I want you to know that I think you did a wonderful job," he continues. "And as for what Oxford might think... well, he's a pompous oaf. We've had half a dozen complaints about a large animal at the zoo and he's ignored all of my warnings. I've visited him on numerous occasions to insist he shut down that project."

"Oh?"

He nods. "Let's just say... if someone were to have released Project Fusion into the wild, so it could live free and away from everything, then I would be okay with that."

Jerry's mouth hangs open. "You would?"

"Absolutely. An animal like that doesn't deserve to be in a cage. I would have done the same in your position... err, had you actually done that. Of course you didn't, though."

You smile slyly. "Of course not, sir."

92

The Captain puts his arm around your shoulder and leads you back to the van. "Regardless, I think two promotions are in order."

Jerry coughs. "Two? You're promoting Rodriguez all the way up to *Captain?*"

He laughs. "No, Holman. She's getting that Lieutenant promotion, and *you* are also getting bumped up to Sergeant."

Jerry trips over himself and falls face-first in the mud. Laughing, you help him up. "You ought to watch where you step, *dude*."

He wipes away the mud. "Hey! Don't call me that!"

"And Lieutenant," Beckett adds. "When we do get back to my office, I want to hear the *real* story. All of it. Just between us."

You and Jerry share a look. "I think we can do that."

CONGRATULATIONS!
YOU HAVE REACHED THE ULTIMATE ENDING!

In recognition for taking up the gauntlet, let it be known to fellow adventurers that you are hereby granted the title of:

Executive Animal Adjudicator!

You may go here: **www.ultimateendingbooks.com/extras.php** and enter code:

JL48841

for tons of extras, and to print out your Ultimate Ending Book Four certificate!

And for a special sneak peek of Ultimate Ending Book 5, *TURN TO PAGE 169*

93

The laughing sound slowly grows louder as you stomp along the trail. You steal a glance behind you and see them following twenty feet behind. They're bounding along lazily, hardly exerting themselves. It's a game to them.

"We need to get safe, fast!"

"I'd love nothing more," Jerry says between gasps, "but what do you suggest?"

The trees are tall and thick, with no low branches to climb. You might be able to shimmy up one, *maybe*, but you'd need to throw down your gun. And then you'd just be trapped.

But what other alternative is there?

"Hey!" Jerry points. "Look!"

Ahead of you the path ends at a chain link fence with a gate. With a rush of hope you sprint faster, sliding to a stop in front.

The gate is barred with a padlock the size of a baseball glove.

"What now?" Jerry asks.

"Only one thing to do." You toss your rifle through the gap in the gate and begin climbing. Jerry is quick behind you.

The hyenas begin barking as they approach, angry with your escape. One of them leaps into the air but slams into the fence just below your feet. It tries again but still misses, its teeth snapping through open air.

When you reach the top you jump the ten feet back down to the ground. Jerry lands on his back clumsily. "Oof!"

Grab your rifle and *TURN TO PAGE 138*

94

The tree is drawing near. You've got a twenty foot lead on the hippo, so if you time it right you should be able to scamper up a branch and into safety.

Ten steps. Five. Zero.

You leap with all your strength, your fingers slapping against the branch. Your fingers stick! A boot scrapes against the trunk and you pull yourself up. Although you think you're safe, you quickly reach for the next branch to put more distance between yourself and the pachyderm.

THWACK.

The entire tree is shaken just before you grab the next branch. Without a grip your feet slip on the wet branch and suddenly you're falling. Your back slams into the branch and you roll, throwing your hands out, desperate to grab onto anything. Your fingers scrape against wet, smooth bark. You're going to fall...

Your arm wraps around the branch, stopping your descent. You're able to crawl back onto the branch and climb higher, this time being more careful of your grip.

When you feel safe enough you stop and look down. The hippo is far below you, stomping around like it owns the place. Though as far as you know, it *is* his place. After snorting at the air he wanders back in the direction of the water.

The rain is still coming down, but it's muted inside the tree's foliage. The leaves also make it difficult to see very far in any other direction.

"Jerry?" you whisper into the radio on your shoulder. "Err, officer Holman. Report, officer Holman."

Silence.

What are you going to do? Sit in the tree *ON PAGE 82*

95

You grab the tray of fish. Cats like fish, right?

As you turn you see that two of the lions have already entered the room, heads hanging low, steps slow and careful. The lead lion's mouth is open is a wicked snarl.

With a heave you upend the tray. Fish and ice slide across the floor. There's only one exit, and it's blocked by the lions, so there's nothing for you to do but watch.

The first animal steps forward and lowers its nose, sniffing the nearest fish. Its tongue flicks out, brushing against its scales. It sniffs some more. The other cats approach. It's working!

The cat takes a step back and shakes its head.

Uh oh.

You try to side-step to the right, but the lions are already picking their way through the ice toward you. Any second now they'll pounce. They're big. It will be easy for them.

You slide down onto your ankles and begin to whimper. Maybe they'll take pity on you. Or maybe it won't matter at all. You never even got to find out what Project Fusion was. No, in that blocked-off room the only thing you've found is...

THE END

96

You follow Jerry across the field and toward the structure, which you realize is a building. You slip inside and close the door.

"This is the building I wanted to go to in the first place," you say. "I called out when we were running from the hippo..."

"I heard," Jerry said. "I just wanted to come around from the side, to try to confuse the hippo."

"Oh."

He frowns at you. "What'd you see back there? On the lions?"

You take a moment to wipe all the mud off your uniform. "They all had their hips shaved," you say. "With big, red injection points in their skin."

"So?"

"I've seen someone donate bone marrow before. It's in the same spot, up by the hip in the pelvis. That's what it reminded me of."

Jerry gives you a level look. "Why would the zoo need lion bone marrow?"

You shake your head. "I don't know. It's probably stupid. I just thought of it."

He shrugs. "This is where I got the steaks. Maybe we can take a quick look around the office before heading on?"

Inspect the empty lion enclosure *ON PAGE 73*

97

"That guy Dave sounds like a friend of mine," Jerry says as you walk back into the cavernous room. "Always pulling pranks. Joking on people. He'd do that kind of thing, changing up the codes..."

Your arm brushes against one of the desks and tears a hole in your uniform. "What the..." You stop and look. There are two sharp objects sticking out of the wood in the side of the desk. You pull one loose. It's two inches long, curved and sharp at one end.

"That's a talon," Jerry says.

You can see that he's right. "It's awfully sharp. Tore a hole right in my uniform."

"Always worrying about that uniform," Jerry mutters.

"I like to appear presentable," you say defensively. "But that's not what I mean. Why is it here, sticking in the desk? It's as if the bird swooped down and tried to grab something, but missed and got it stuck in the wood."

PLOP.

You both whirl. "What was that?"

"I don't know."

PLOP.

This time you see it happen. A long stream of goop fell from the sky, landing in a puddle on the ground. Adding to the already thick layer of dropping everywhere.

"Uh oh." You and Jerry share a look of fear.

Look up *ON PAGE 12*

98

The brush parts and four dog-like creatures stalk out. Their legs are double-jointed, and they have a stubby, snout-like face with round ears. Their skin is yellowish with dark spots.

"Those are hyenas!" Jerry says.

They spread out in a line, all four facing you. At first they seem curious, inspecting the two-legged strangers. Then one of them growls.

"Can we outrun them?" you whisper.

"I don't know. I doubt it."

You look at your rifle. The first shot will be easy, but then you will need to quickly load another dart into the chamber before shooting again. You and Jerry would need to both make two perfect shots.

He lifts his rifle slowly and glances at you. Waiting for your command.

FLIP TWO COINS! How many times did it land tails?

If it landed tails 0 times, *GO TO PAGE 153*
If it landed tails 1 time, *GO TO PAGE 63*
If it landed tails 2 times, *GO TO PAGE 69*

Alternatively, *RUN AWAY TO PAGE 166*

99

The spiders inch closer, each long leg carefully picking across the floor. For some reason you get the impression they're hungry.

"I can't wait for you Jerry!"

"Just another second! Hold on, I–"

You can't stand it anymore. Throwing your flashlight at them, you bolt across the room to your right, in the opposite direction of the office door. You can't hear the spiders over the sound of your metal flashlight rolling around, but you think you can hear Jerry calling from the office.

You follow the wall for fifty feet until it ends at a corner. You begin to turn to follow that until something wet grabs your foot. The ground flies up to smack you in the face.

Oof.

For a long moment you can't see anything. Your vision goes from ultra-bright back to darkness, and then you realize that's how the room is supposed to look.

You try to roll over but something is stopping you. Your ankle can't move. You twist to see, and realize there's a greyish glob of goo wrapped around your ankle. It feels sticky to the touch, and oddly familiar. You realize it's a giant wad of spiderwebbing just as four shadows close in.

"Jerry!"

You hear him coming, but it's too late. The spiders as big as dogs leap like dogs too, landing on you and moving you with their legs. They break your ankle free and spin you like a drill, wrapping you as they go. You try to call out for your partner again but now the webbing is in your mouth.

The last thing you see is Jerry bravely kicking at the spiders with his boot, before the web covers your eyes. You can sense that he's still fighting, but for you this is...

THE END

100

With slow steps that make no noise on the metal floor, you walk out onto the balcony. You crane your head to look up on the roof as you go farther out. It's dark, but you still don't see anything.

You reach the edge of the railing, which gives you a view of most of the roof. You definitely don't see anything.

"Did it fly away?" Jerry whispers.

"I don't know."

In front of you is a staircase leading up to the roof. There's a gate at the entrance with a sign that says "Tower Token Required" in big elaborate writing.

"It flew away," Jerry decides. "There's nothing more for us to do. Let's get out of here."

But then a dark shape swings into view, a black splotch against an even darker sky. You and Jerry both draw in your breath at the same time.

This is it. Take down Project Fusion *ON PAGE 123*

101

You gladly take his hand and allow him to pull you to your feet. "What was that?"

He grins. "Subsonic interference device," he says.

You give him a blank stare. "Don't tell me you understand what that series of words means."

He laughs and holds out his other hand. There's a small oval device in his palm, like a garage door opener. "No, I don't. But it was on the wall in there. Glad you listened to me!"

"If it was on the wall, what took you so long to use it?" Those spiders had nearly jumped you!

"Hey, the battery wasn't working. Had to find a replacement in the drawer." He smirks. "It worked, didn't it?"

You're still shaken, but glad to have a partner with you. "Yeah, you're right."

"Oh," he adds, "and I found this." He hands you a card. Written on the front, in indented letters, are the words:

WARDEN HUT CODE: 122

"Not too shabby, partner," you admit. You stick it in your pocket. "But we're going to need this later, so you'd better let me hold onto it."

He looks offended. "I'm not that clumsy."

Now it's your turn to smile. "I saw you lose your sunglasses while they were on your face!"

"I forgot, is all..."

You slap him on the shoulder. "Either way, you're right. We need some of those tranquilizer darts."

Head back outside *ON PAGE 75*

102

"Come on," you say. "Let's get these tranquilizer darts once and for all."

Jerry moans as you take off down the path, but you hear him follow nonetheless.

The rain is coming down harder, making the stone path slick. Your boots echo off the trees. You feel like you're too loud. Although there's no sign of whatever that thing was, you still feel awfully exposed out there. Vulnerable. Maybe this wasn't such a good idea after all.

You reach the fallen tree across the path. Ducking down to pass underneath, you look back at Jerry. He's twenty feet behind. "Come on, I thought you were faster than this."

The sound of a thick tree cracking comes from the woods to the right. You have just enough time to grab Jerry and slide under the fallen tree before another one comes toppling across the path. The trees bounce and flex from all the weight, knocking you down onto the wet path.

Another screech cuts the air. This time it sounds like it's only a few feet away.

The two trees provide a protected canopy, but also block your view. You can hear the animal stomping around. The rain drizzles down between the wood around you as you listen.

"We have to move," you say. "We can't stay here."

"We shouldn't have run out here..."

One of the heavy paving stones has come loose. You pick it up. "I'm going to throw this into the woods behind us. Hopefully it distracts that *thing* long enough for us to get away."

"You think that will work?"

"Do you have a better idea?"

Hopefully you're lucky.

Roll a die (or pick a number at random):

If you rolled a 1 or 6, *FLIP TO PAGE 56*
If you rolled a 2, 3, 4, or 5, *GO TO PAGE 136*

103

You didn't come this far just to turn around now. That Lieutenant promotion is as good as yours. You just need to push a little farther.

The scaffolding tilts precariously as you climb the ladder to the final platform. You stay on your knees once there, to keep your balance more easily. The open window into the dome is just above your eyesight.

The growling sound has stopped. In fact, it seems awfully quiet now that you're up there. Like you've stumbled upon a bear cave and disturbed the beast. *They're just birds*, you think, but it's a weak defense. You remember the claws of the hawk swooping down on you inside the dome.

You inch toward the open window to peer inside, hoping that the bird with the code attached to its claw is close. Slowly, like a predator, you raise your eyes above the lip.

The inside of the dome is pitch black. Your eyes adjust after a moment and you can make out the metal rafters criss-crossing the ceiling, now at eye-level. Dark shapes perch throughout the space.

Something growls.

It's to the right, just inside the window. You turn and look in that direction. At first you don't see anything, just a mass of black, but then you realize you're looking at one large object. One large *thing.*

And as your eyes adjust further, you see two big, hairy, paws. Like cat paws, only massive.

"What the..." you mutter.

All of a sudden the huge animal moves. It's coming right at you!

Say your prayers *ON PAGE 124*

104

"Hey, you're right," you suddenly remember. "The Visitor Center said we need a Tower Token to get to the top."

"So where do we get one?"

The sign next to the path has arrows leading in two directions. To the left is the Bear Abode. To the right in the Snake Sanctuary.

Do you have the code to get into either?

If you have the Bear Abode Code, *TURN TO THAT PAGE*
If you have the Snake Sanctuary Code, *GO TO THAT PAGE*
If you have neither, *TURN TO PAGE 140*

105

You punch 1-0-5 into the keypad. The door opens horizontally.

The room is cavernous, with bird exhibits and information in little stands all around the floor. Cages are spaced every twenty feet, with guide ropes surrounding them to keep people from getting too close. High above you is the top of the dome, with strange dark tiles instead of glass like on the outside.

"There's the office," Jerry says, pointing across the room.

You take a step forward and your foot sinks into something. "What the..."

"Eww," Jerry says. "What is it?"

You realize what it is. The floor is covered in a layer of bird droppings. Every inch of the huge room.

You make your way across the floor, wincing with each disgusting step. As you pass a bird cage you realize the bars have been bent open on the side, creating a hole large enough for the bird–a turkey vulture, the sign informs you–to fly out. "That explains all the droppings."

"I don't know how the zookeepers do it. I couldn't deal with cleaning up poop all day."

"What about your daughter Amy?"

"What about her?"

"Well," you say, "don't you have to clean her diaper?"

Jerry thinks about that for a minute. "I still don't like it," he finally says.

You reach the office door. Thankfully there's no keycode required, and the door opens at your touch.

106

Although devoid of bird droppings, the office is considerably messier than the one in the Monkey Manor. Papers everywhere, a desk lamp on its side. The computer chair has been flipped over and one of the wheels is missing.

"Looks like a fight broke out," Jerry says.

"Yeah, it does."

The computer has no power, which isn't a surprise. But sitting on the keyboard is a printed-out email conversation:

Debbie,

You need a better sense of humor. Sure, I changed the code to the Power Station, but it's easy to figure out. I even made it into a math problem so someone as boring as you could get it. The code is: 4, plus the number of monkeys in the Monkey Manor, divided by 4, multiplied by the number of pandas at the zoo. See? Simple!

-Dave

"That Dave guy sounds like a jerk," you say.

Jerry nods. "At least we have the code. Now we can turn the power on. *Finally.*"

"Yeah, but the riddle. How many pandas are here? The Panda Palace is on the other side..."

Jerry quiets you with a wave. "There are two pandas at the zoo, a male and a female. It was in the front office when we entered the park. Did you catch how many monkeys were at the Monkey Manor?"

You nod. "I think so."

"Then let's head back to the Power Station and do the math there."

Exit back into the dome room *ON PAGE 97*

107

"Jerry, why didn't you say that when we were out there?"

He smiles weakly. "It's over in the corner, by one of the big tanks. I didn't want to go near it."

You go back into the lobby area and see the glowing green screen in the far corner. You approach it and smile. "Well good. All we have–"

You realize Jerry is still over by the door to the office. "I'm safe over here," he calls. "I'll watch your back."

Chuckling to yourself, you look at the screen. There's a trivia question listed:

*The **Coral Snake** and **King Snake** may look very similar, but there are subtle differences in the colors. Which of the two is venemous?*

"Jerry, do you remember the answer to this trivia question? We saw the answer when we entered the park."

"I don't know," he says. "I'm going to stay over here. You've got it, partner!"

You take a deep breath and read the question again.

Do you know the answer?

To answer **Coral Snake,** *TURN TO PAGE 164*
To answer **King Snake,** *FLIP TO PAGE 17*

109

Your hand slowly leaves the radio as you turn around. A single lion stands before you, mouth open in a silent snarl.

"Hey there, buddy," you whisper, taking a step back.

The lion growls again. You're not entire sure what to do, so you keep backing away slowly.

The lion begins sniffing the air, as if wondering what you are. If you'll be tasty.

Time to make a decision. Do you grab your pepper spray and hope it's enough to stop a 300 pound cat, or do you turn and run?

There's a reason you carry it around. Grab the pepper spray *ON PAGE 112*
Running is the only smart choice. Do it *ON PAGE 121*

110

The code works and the door opens. Afraid that it might suddenly close again, you and Jerry jump inside.

The interior of the Power Station is one large room with computers and electrical equipment all along the walls. Half the room shines with glowing buttons and lights, like a thousand colorful, flickering stars.

The other half of the room is dark.

"Looks like that's the side we need to turn back on," you say.

Jerry chuckles. "What gave you that idea?"

Ignoring his sarcasm, you approach the dark wall of computer equipment. Three huge levers attached to box-like protrusions stick out from the wall. All three are currently in the down position.

There's a post-it note attached to the wall. You remove it and read:

To reboot system: engage Lever 1 (primary computer system), wait 10 seconds, then engage Lever 2 (exterior enclosure power), wait 10 seconds, then engage Lever 3 (ancillary computer network).

You look at the wall of levers. They're in order: 1-2-3.

Jerry looks at the note. "Pretty simple. What are you waiting for?"

To engage the levers in that order (1-2-3), *GO TO PAGE 128*
To engage the levers in REVERSE order (3-2-1), *GO TO PAGE 133*

111

POP.

The dart hisses through the air, pink feathers the only thing keeping it visible. You hold your breath as it arcs toward the Tower, toward the beast you were sent to subdue.

And zips just by the animal's head, landing somewhere on the other side.

"No!" Jerry cries, throwing down his rifle. "I was so close!"

The shot disturbed the animal. It shifts as if turning to look down at you, though you can't make out any part of its body.

It screeches, a terrifying sound of fury.

Now what happens? *TURN TO PAGE 139*

112

Your hand goes to your belt to grab your pepper spray... but it's not there.

It must have fallen off my belt in the water.

Oh no.

Not that it would probably help. This cat looks angry, and you've fallen right into its territory. Better turn and...

Another sound comes from behind. You whirl and see two more lions, circling you from the other side. Cutting off your escape.

Surrounding you.

"Just great," you mutter. "I always wanted a cat, but not like this. As a pet!"

Your joke doesn't sway them. The first lion takes a step forward with one of its massive paws.

Find out if you're kibble *ON PAGE 130*

113

You shake your head. "You've seen all these Zoo Announcements. Project Fusion, whatever it is, is the most important thing at the zoo. If we bring it under control we'll be heroes!"

"But the note says..."

"The note says not to come within 50 feet," you say. "We'll keep our distance. You can hit it from that far, right?"

He draws himself up indignantly. "I'm the best Marksman the Academy has seen in thirty years. Of course I can."

"Then there's no problem, is there?"

Jerry grumbles but then nods.

You head deeper into the park toward the Observation Tower. A gazelle appears around a bend, eating some grass next to the road. You slow down enough for Jerry to aim and fire a dart. It catches the animal in the neck. The gazelle wavers and slowly falls to the grass.

"Nice shot!"

He smiles smugly. "I told you!"

You find several other kinds of animals along the way, stopping to gently sedate each one. You begin to feel like you're gaining control of the zoo in earnest.

Until you hear a strange sound coming from the trees to your right.

"What's that?"

You cock your ears, listening. "It almost sounds like... laughter."

Jerry tenses. "Uh oh. I think I know what those are."

The bushes shake.

Raise your rifles *ON PAGE 98*

114

The eyes drift forward, suspended in the darkness. You get the distinct impression they're stalking you. Cutting off your escape.

Lightning flashes outside, giving a brief view of the room.

115

The lions are slightly larger than dogs, with yellowish fur and a long tail. Another flash of lightning shows them again. They're definitely surrounding you. You're about to be out of options.

Since the door outside is now blocked, you slip through the other direction, with Jerry close on your heels. There's an interior doorway–with no door–leading into a preparation area. You recognize it as a room where zoo employees might get food ready for the animals. The ground is still cement, but there are some steel tables, and a refrigerator in the corner.

A growl sounds behind you.

Thinking fast, you throw open the door to the fridge. There are two big trays of food: the left has stacks of fish on ice, the right has raw steaks, juicy and red. The trays are big, so it'll take both of you to lift it out.

"Which food do we grab?" Jerry asks.

To take the fish, *GO TO PAGE 95*
To take the steaks, *GO TO PAGE 68*

116

You rush down to the path just as a line of black, windowless vans comes roaring around the corner and into the clearing. One by one they zoom past and halt at the base of the Observation Tower. You and Jerry share a look.

The door to the first van opens. You immediately recognize the two bars on the man's uniform. Indicating the rank of Captain.

You scramble forward and salute. "Captain Beckett, sir!"

Jerry is still standing there, holding the tranquilizer rifle. Only when you clear your throat does he jump next to you and mimic the salute.

Captain Beckett eyes the two of you. He's a bull of a man, sixty years old with broad shoulders and muscular arms. His uniform is tight and orderly, his face chiseled with discipline.

"Sir," you begin, "a status update. We have–"

He silences you with a hand and points up to the tower. "There was just an animal there. A *special* animal. What happened to it?"

"Uhh." You're not sure what to say. "Well..."

117

Another man hops out of the passenger side of the first van. He looks like Teddy Roosevelt come alive: tan safari uniform, round spectacles, and reddish mustache.

"It's gone! Where did it go?" He looks at you and Jerry, and the tranquilizer rifles on the ground. "Did you get it?"

The Captain clears his throat. "Rodriguez, Holman. Meet Warden Oxford. He runs the zoo."

"So we've heard," Jerry mutters.

"Unfortunately we did not get the animal," you explain. "We saw your Zoo Announcement advising to stay beyond 50 feet from Project Fusion. Since it took up a position at the top of the Tower we decided our only course of action was to attempt to shoot it from here." You hesitate for a moment. "Officer Holman was out of tranquilizer darts, so I took the shot. I missed, and the beast flew away to the west."

Jerry gawks at you. "Dude..."

You silence him with a stare.

The Warden bristles. "Project Fu... err, that *animal* is supposed to be classified. You're not supposed to know its name, or anything about it." He takes a long look at you and casually adds, "I don't suppose you saw it up close, did you?"

"No sir. Only from a distance."

He stared a moment longer as if deciding if you're telling the truth. "Fine. I'm extremely disappointed in your results here, officers. Beckett, I thought you sent your department's finest?"

"These are my finest officers," Beckett says gruffly.

A steady *THUMP THUMP THUMP* cuts the air. Moments later two military-style helicopters burst into view, shooting over you into the area above the Observation Tower. They circle around in opposite directions, shining spotlights down on the top of the Tower.

Oxford blows out his mustache. "Hrmm. Well then. I will discuss this more with you in the morning, Beckett." He turns away and pulls out a walkie talkie. "Call off the birds. It's not on the Tower anymore. The police officers scared it away..."

You groan inwardly. This was your chance and you completely blew it.

118

You turn to the Captain. "Sir. I accept full responsibility for this failure."

Captain Beckett cranes his neck to stare up at the Tower. "Huh huh. You're telling me you attempted a shot from so far away, Rodriguez?"

Hesitating only a split second, you say, "Yes, sir."

He looks at Jerry. "Officer Holman, is this true?"

"I, err, uhh..." he sputters. He looks at you.

Captain Beckett laughs. "Come on now. Jerry is the best marksman in the precinct, and he's not shy about letting people know. He took the shot, didn't he?"

Sheepishly, you nod your head.

"That's a mature thing to do, Rodriguez. Taking responsibility instead of blaming your partner."

It almost sounds like he's happy, in spite of everything. "Sir?"

"Warden Oxford is a pompous oaf. He lost control of this zoo and called in a favor to have me help him. Well I'm pleased with how you two performed. You kept many of the animals from escaping, and even attempted to sedate Oxford's *science project*, despite all warnings and fears. I don't care if he's unhappy. Let him worry about that animal."

He puts an arm around your shoulder and leads you away. "The way an officer performs under pressure is more important than the end result. You made some good decisions tonight, Rodriguez. Now let's talk about that Lieutenant position..."

THE END

119

You pull out a card from your pocket. "I've got the Snake Sanctuary Code right here."

Jerry turns a shade of white. "Uhh... do we have to go there?"

"If we want to get the Tower Token, then yes we do."

He looks like he wants to throw up, but he nods. "Okay. You, uhh, lead the way."

You follow the path and come to the Snake Sanctuary, a dark building with no windows. You punch 1-1-9 into the keypad and the door opens.

Your boots make very little noise as you stalk inside, flashlight pointed ahead of you. Rows of glass tanks line each wall, with glowing sunlamps inside. You move the flashlight around each wall, checking every single cage.

What you see makes you relax. "Hey Jerry, it's okay. It's clean in here. None of the tanks are broken."

Jerry steps inside cautiously, as if he doesn't believe you. "I still don't like snakes," he squeaks.

"That's fine. Just stay in the center of the room and watch my back while I search the office."

"I think I'd rather stay close to you, if that's okay." Jerry is standing so close you can smell his breath.

Laughing, you say, "Okay, follow me then."

Search the office *ON PAGE 70*

120

You race back to the Power Station. Jerry grabs the piece of paper and reads it off again.

"*The code is: 4, plus the number of monkeys in the Monkey Manor, divided by 4, multiplied by the number of pandas at the zoo.*" He looks at you. "There are two pandas in the zoo, I know that for sure."

You wrinkle your face. "And the number of monkeys in the Monkey Manor..." You think back, remembering the sign outside.

Can you figure it out?

If you know the answer, solve the riddle and *TURN TO THAT PAGE*

Otherwise, run back to the Monkey Manor *ON PAGE 51*

121

This is really stupid. The cat is enormous, easily larger than you. There's no point trying to fight it unless you absolutely have to. Time to run away.

But before you have a chance to run, another sound comes from behind. You whirl and see two more lions, circling you from the other side. Cutting off your escape.

Surrounding you.

"So much for that," you mutter. Your hand goes to your belt to grab the pepper spray.

It's gone.

It must have fallen off my belt in the water. That's the only explanation.

The first lion takes a step forward with one of its massive paws.

Discover your fate *ON PAGE 130*

122

You punch the code into the keypad. There's a pause, then a beep, and then the door hisses open.

Some emergency lights recessed in the ceiling bathe the square room in red. It's an armory, with racks of rifles along one wall, and a table with cattle prods and other zoo equipment. A row of lockers lines another wall with various types of suits and uniforms.

You step up to the first table and find a note from the Warden.

ZOO ANNOUNCEMENT.

Do not, I repeat, DO NOT, under any circumstances, approach Project Fusion within 50 feet. It moves extremely fast and without warning, so anything closer than that is too dangerous. Keep a wide range, guys. I mean it. Be safe.

-Warden Oxford

"Easier said than done," Jerry mutters.

Grab some firepower *ON PAGE 144*

123

The shadow stops moving. It's just a silhouette, but you get the impression it's sitting down. Even from this distance, about 50 feet away, it's huge.

For a long moment you and Jerry stand there, frozen.

Slowly, inch by inch, Jerry raises his rifle. He levels it at the dark beast and takes a long breath. "Give the order," he whispers.

The animal isn't moving. It's 50 feet away. This is the best chance you're going to get. You glance at the stairs leading up to the top, and the "Tower Token Required" sign.

To order Jerry to fire, roll a die (or pick a number at random):

If you rolled a 1 or 2, *TURN TO PAGE 111*
If you rolled a 3, 4, 5, or 6, *GO TO PAGE 165*

OR, if you have the Tower Token and want to climb onto the roof, *GO TO PAGE 159*

124

The huge beast charges, lunging at the window. Moving on instinct alone, you duck down between the window and the scaffolding.

The glass shatters and rains down on you. There's a rush of wind above you, like an industrial fan blowing across your back. A shriek cuts the sky, and for a brief heartbeat you're certain you're going to die.

Yet the noise and air moves on, the flapping of wings now farther away. You look up and see a dark silhouette moving across the sky on massive wings. It lilts as it flies, constantly rising and dropping as if it's injured. It disappears over the treetops.

"What was that?" Jerry yells.

You glance back at the window. The animal shattered the glass all around it when it exited, creating a hole ten feet across. What kind of bird is that big?

And the paws. You were certain those were paws with fur on them, but now you aren't so sure. Maybe the darkness played a trick on you.

"I don't know," you begin to tell Jerry, but then you cut off.

The hawk that swooped down on you is directly in front of you, perched just inside the window. And stuck to his talon is a white piece of paper.

The Power Station code!

125

"Rodriguez?" Jerry yells. "Rodriguez, what's going on?"

Ignoring him, you lean toward the bird. It's facing you with his head cocked, as if he's curious. *Please don't move,* you beg. *Don't attack me. Just stay there for another second.* Its dark eyes watch you draw near.

Slowly you reach forward. Your finger grabs the paper.

The bird darts forward, feathers flying all around. You fall backwards onto the scaffolding platform as the hawk takes to the air, flying to freedom.

"Rodriguez? Katy? Dude, this isn't funny. Say something!"

You roll over and peer down at your partner. You thrust the paper out to him. "I got the code. And don't call me dude!"

By the time you reach the ground all the birds inside the dome are now flying out of the dome, a stream of feathers exiting the hole. "What was that thing?" Jerry asks. "Was it Project..."

"I don't know," you cut him off. "All that matters is we got the code. Let's go turn the power on!"

Head back to the Power Station *ON PAGE 120*

126

There's a direct path from the Power Station to the Warden Hut, but it's *long*. You walk for ten minutes, winding a round the tall Observation Tower at the center of the zoo. "We would already have some shiny new tranquilizer rifles in our hands if we had gone to the Warden Hut first," Jerry says in the dark silence of the path.

"How do you know they're shiny and new?"

"I don't know. But we would have them." He looks at the tall trees all around. "And then I wouldn't be walking along, afraid of what might jump out at me."

"I'm not afraid," you say with just a hint of mocking. "Maybe you need some courage? Like the Cowardly Lion?"

"I'm just saying," he mutters.

You pat him on the back reassuringly. "Relax. Things are going well. We've contained several animal enclosures to the best of our abilities, have restored power to the park, and are heading to the Warden Hut now. Why do you have to be so negative?"

Somewhere distant, an animal roars.

It's a high-pitched sound, like a bird's shriek but with more muscle behind it. The tail end of the sound echoes for a few moments.

"That's why," Jerry says, meeting your gaze.

You walk in silence for a bit.

"I still wonder what it is," you say. "The footprints in the mud, and what we saw at the Bird Bastion... I swear it has paws like a cat."

"That's crazy," Jerry says. "It can fly. What kind of animal has cat paws and can fly? Oh, and is the size of a school bus?"

He's right, but you still can't shake that feeling...

A building appears ahead. "Finally," Jerry says. "The Warden Hut."

TURN TO PAGE 160

"I trust your aim," you say. "Officer Holman, please attempt to subdue that creature from here."

His face grows serious. "Yes ma'am."

He takes aim, pointing the rifle practically vertical in the air. Project Fusion, whatever it is, shifts high above but stays in view.

Jerry takes a deep breath.

Roll a die (or pick a number at random):

If you rolled a 1 or 2, *TURN TO PAGE 158*
If you rolled a 3 or 4, *TURN TO PAGE 149*
If you rolled a 5 or 6, *TURN TO PAGE 111*

128

"Yep, pretty simple," you agree. "Want to do the honors?"

Jerry shakes his head. "All you."

You approach the first panel. The lever has two bars, sort of like how an aircraft accelerator looks.

"Here goes." You grab it with both hands and push it toward the ceiling.

KA-CHUNK.

The mechanical sound echoes in the room for an instant, and then the entire panel lights up. The hum of machinery comes from deep within the wall. Lights blink everywhere, mostly red and yellow. Slowly they start turning green. You take that as a good sign.

"Six, seven, eight..." you count. At ten you throw the second switch. Another sound like a generator whines and more flashing indicators come to life. Easy as pie.

You count to ten again and throw the final switch.

You aren't sure what happened, but something smashes into your back. Everything is *really* bright for a while, and you can't seem to see anything. There's a strange burning smell too. Slowly the light fades and you see Jerry standing over you.

"Rodriguez? Rodriguez!"

He's yelling, dim at first but then louder as your hearing returns. You open your mouth to speak but only a squeak comes out.

You reach up and try to touch Jerry. That's when you see your arm. Your uniform is burned to a crisp and smoking.

"Rodriguez, you were electrocuted!"

You don't feel too bad, but Jerry insists you stay put. Now that the power is back on he uses the phone to call Captain Beckett. He's arguing with the Captain, so you can tell he's unhappy. "You'll get that promotion another time," Jerry says when he returns. "They'll be here soon."

It's too bad, because you still want to push on, to try to do your job. But deep down you know you can't, because you've reached...

THE END

129

You shake your head. "You've seen all these Zoo Announcements. Project Fusion, whatever it is, is the most important thing at the zoo. If we bring it under control we'll be heroes!"

"But the note says..."

"The note says not to come within 50 feet," you say. "We'll keep our distance. You can hit it from that far, right?"

He draws himself up indignantly. "I'm the best Marksman the Academy has seen in thirty years. Of course I can."

"Then there's no problem, is there?"

Jerry grumbles but climbs up in the seat, his upper body sticking through the sun roof. "Just drive."

You head deeper into the park toward the Observation Tower. A gazelle appears around a bend, eating some grass next to the road. You slow down enough for Jerry to aim and fire a dart. It catches the animal in the neck. The gazelle wavers and slowly falls to the grass.

"Nice shot!"

He smiles smugly. "I told you!"

You find several other kinds of animals along the way, including a pack of hyenas. You slow down so Jerry can feather them with darts before continuing on. After a few more minutes of shooting you say, "Hey, how much ammo do you have?"

There's a pause while Jerry looks. "Uhh."

"What is it?"

"Looks like I only have one dart left."

"Just one? Jerry!"

"Sorry! I was having fun sedating the animals."

"Well, one will have to do. Let's just hope it's enough for that big animal." You glance up at your partner. "And let's hope you don't miss."

"Hey! I haven't missed yet!"

The Observation Tower grows larger as you near.

It's go time. *TURN TO PAGE 156*

130

The first cat comes within a few feet of you before stopping. It crouches down, about to strike. Its mouth opens, showing rows of sharp teeth.

"HEY!"

A voice cuts the night off to the left. "Jerry?"

"HEY YOU BIG DUMB CATS!" he screams, coming into the field. "YEAH YOU GUYS! SHE'S NOT VERY TASTY! LEAVE HER ALONE!"

He has something in his arms, like a big plastic tray. The cats turn toward him, but are still surrounding you.

Jerry drops the tray into the mud. With a confident flourish he reaches down and removes a thick, red steak. "This is much tastier than officer Rodriguez over there!" He waves it tauntingly.

That got the lions' attention. They paw toward him, abandoning you altogether.

He throws the first steak on the ground. It's immediately scooped up by the closest lion. He throws three more in the area between them and the tray and they pounce, now fighting over the food. He uses the opportunity to slip away from them. You quietly meet him over on the side as they tear into the food, knocking the tray over and splashing in the mud.

"Thank me later," he says, giving you a big grin. "But for now, let's go!"

Something on the back of one of the lions catches your attention. Its fur has been shaved from its hip, up near where it meets its tail. After a few seconds you realize all three lions are that way.

"What do you think..." you begin.

"Rodriguez, COME ON!" He grabs your arm.

He's right, it's time to *go.* *RUN TO PAGE 96*

131

After succeeding once, timing the dive is easy. Just before the hawk's razor-sharp talons come within reach, you throw yourself flat, sliding through the wet, white muck.

The bird zooms past. Jerry dives out of the way even though the bird isn't coming after him. For a moment you laugh.

The hawk begins climbing back toward the ceiling, and you're not going to give it a chance to attack a third time. Scrambling to your feet you sprint for the door, grabbing Jerry's arm and pulling him along with you. The two of you fall through the door into the cool evening air, closing the door behind you.

You sit on the ground for a long while, breathing heavily, reveling in your escape.

Catch your breath *ON PAGE 137*

132

"Lucky we found the code on the way here," you say. "One-three-two."

The keypad makes a low beep of denial.

"Huh." You enter the code again, and it makes the same noise.

"What are you doing wrong?" Jerry asks.

"Nothing. All I'm doing is punching in the code!"

"Let me try." He shoulders you out of the way and thumbs the numbers into the pad. Nothing.

"Told you."

"Well then what are we supposed to do?" he asks. "I *told you* we should have gone to get the tranquilizer rifles first..."

You look around. "I guess we'll have to figure out another way to turn the power on. Maybe we should explore a different area."

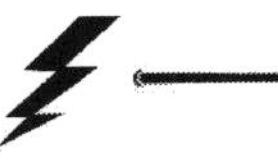

TURN BACK TO PAGE 47

133

"Woah woah woah," you say. "The Zoo Announcement back at the Monkey Manor said Dave reversed the circuits."

"Ohh, right."

"See? This is why you need to stop and think more often, Jerry!"

For once he looks sheepish. "Yeah, you're right. That would have been bad."

You approach the panel. Lever 3 has two bars, sort of like how an aircraft accelerator looks.

"Here goes." You grab it with both hands and push it toward the ceiling.

KA-CHUNK.

The mechanical sound echoes in the room for an instant, and then the entire panel lights up. The hum of machinery comes from deep within the wall. Lights blink everywhere, mostly red and yellow. Slowly they start turning green. You take that as a good sign.

"Six, seven, eight..." you count. At ten you throw Lever 2. Another sound like a generator whines and more flashing indicators come to life. Easy as pie.

You count to ten again and throw Lever 1, wincing with anticipation.

The third panels hums to life normally.

"Whew," you say, relaxing. "I wasn't sure that would work."

"Me neither," Jerry admits. "That's why I let you throw them, not me!"

The power is back on. Form a plan *ON PAGE 141*

134

"We only have one dart," you say, "and we need to make it count. Let's get closer."

"But the Zoo Announcement said not to get within..."

You take your partner by the shoulders. "Jerry, we have to get this thing under control. It's the most important part of the park, whatever it is. If you don't feel comfortable then you can stay down here and I'll take the rifle and go up there by myself."

He steels himself. "No way. We're partners. I'm with you until the end."

You smile. "Glad to hear it!"

Jerry looks around. "Are we sure we have everything we need? Once we go inside we won't have time to come back out before the Animal Control guys arrive."

If you're ready, *CLIMB TO PAGE 140*

If you feel like you're missing something, *GO BACK TO PAGE 104*

135

You follow the path to the Bear Abode, a cement-walled building with a single door entrance. You thumb the code into the keypad and the door beeps and opens, allowing you inside.

A viewing area opens in front of you, with the animal pit beyond. The employee office is to the right though, so you slip inside there.

It's just like all the other offices you've seen so far. A quick search turns up nothing except another message from the Warden:

ZOO ANNOUNCEMENT.

After the incident with Marlene, Project Fusion is hereby closed to all personnel except myself. All feeding will be administered by me, under the strictest of security settings. And don't worry about Marlene–the hospital says the claw marks were not very deep and she is expected to make a full recovery. Please sign the 'Get Well' card for her in my office.

-Warden Oxford

"Claw marks?" Jerry licks his lips nervously. "Are we sure we want to do this?"

You ignore his question, because you're trying to ignore the rising sense of dread in your chest. "There's nothing in here. Let's check the main area."

Go back to the viewing area *ON PAGE 13*

136

You grip the heavy stone in your hand, taking a few breaths to harden your courage. The booming sound of the animal's footsteps is like something out of Jurassic Park.

"On the count of three," you whisper. "One. Two."

"Three!"

You lean out from under the tree and heave the stone into the woods behind you. Not waiting to see what happened, you turn and sprint in the direction of the Warden's Hut.

It gives you a ten second head start. Between the heavy raindrops and the sound of your breathing you can't even hear the beast. For a few, precious, moments you begin to think you'll escape.

Something crashes into your back, throwing you forward. You slide across the path, scraping the buttons on your uniform. A moment later Jerry flies past you too, tumbling to the ground.

"What the..."

You roll over just in time to see a huge shape loom over you. It blocks the rain, but from this angle it's too dark to make much out. For a strange moment the way it sits there reminds you of your sister's cat.

Jerry screams in terror, but a resigned peacefulness comes over you. You think about Captain Beckett and the promotion you were hoping to receive. That's all you wanted, but it looks like you failed.

The animal lifts a massive paw. You wish you had learned more about him, too. Maybe another time, you think, since this is...

THE END

137

Jerry finally opens his mouth, but you cut him off.

"Don't even think about making fun of my dirty uniform," you say. "I don't want to hear it right now."

He closes his mouth.

There's a loud crash high in the sky. You both whip your heads to stare up at the top of the dome, near the scaffolding. A giant animal has smashed through the glass, creating a huge hole in the dome. It's the size of a school bus! The winged beast flies away to the north, in the direction of the Observation Tower. It disappears over the treetops.

"What was that?" you both ask at the same time.

You laugh, because you're too afraid to do anything else.

The paper with the riddle on it is still clutched in your hands. "We were lucky to get out of there," you say. "But I don't think we should stretch our luck any further. Let's go turn the power on, and then I want to get those tranquilizers."

Jerry grins. "Rodriguez, you're finally starting to make sense."

Go back to the Power Station *ON PAGE 120*

138

You grab your rifle and aim at the fence, just in case the hyenas find a way through. Enraged, they throw themselves at the fence over and over. It heaves and shakes but holds strong.

Jerry picks up his gun and fires, catching one in the thigh and causing it to wobble and slump to the ground. You fire at another but miss.

The other hyenas, confused, quickly flee back into the woods.

You sigh. "That was... intense."

"Yeah." He looks around. "The Observation Tower is that way. Let's follow the fence in that direction. Maybe there will be an exit."

You walk along in silence, wondering what kind of enclosure you're in. It's awfully quiet in this area, minus the hyenas. Maybe they've scared everything off. Or maybe they've had many of the other zoo animals for lunch. You hope that's not the case or Captain Beckett will *not* be happy.

Either way, you enjoy the silence as you walk along.

Until there's another noise ahead, behind some bushes.

You raise your rifle and load another dart, but your fingers are so frantic that the needle breaks off inside. "Oh no!" you yell.

Jerry is quickly trying to load his own. The bushes shake violently. "It's coming!"

Meet your end *ON PAGE 143*

139

With a *whoosh* of air the animal leaps from the Tower. For an agonizing moment you're afraid it's going to dive down on you and Jerry. You tense, ready to sprint to safety.

But instead it flaps its wings and takes to the sky. It's now obvious that it has some type of injury, flapping uncoordinated and lopsided. It even sounds like it's in pain as it shrieks one final time.

As it disappears over the trees to the west you feel strangely sad. Like you've missed out on something special.

"I'm sorry," Jerry says, looking down at his feet. "I failed. I had one job and I messed it up."

You pat him on the shoulder. "Still a better shot than I would have made."

"You may not be mad," he says, "but it doesn't make me feel any better. It got away because of me."

A sound drifts from the woods, from the road leading toward the park entrance. It almost sounds like cars...

Run and see *ON PAGE 116*

140

"I guess we have everything we need," you say. "It'd be great to go back to the Warden Hut and get more darts, but there's just no time. We have to make this one dart count."

"Good thing I'm the best," Jerry says, hefting his rifle. "Let's go."

You approach the door at the base of the Tower. There's no keypad, and it already stands open. "Finally, we don't need a stupid code."

"Agreed."

Step inside *ON PAGE 154*

141

"So the power is on," you say, walking around the perimeter of the big Power Station room. "That should keep the rest of the animals contained, if they haven't already broken free."

"We still have that Project Fusion thing to worry about," Jerry notes.

You approach a computer desk in the corner. "That's why I want to get those tranquilizer rifles next." A grid of security screens are stacked on the desk, showing video feeds scattered throughout the park. "Speaking of which..."

Jerry steps up next to you and you point to one of the screens. It shows the outside of the Insect Enclosure on the other side of the park. A gaping hole has been ripped in the roof of the two-story building.

Something moves inside, obscured by the shadow. Something big.

"I think that's it," you said. "It's the same thing that flew out of the Bird Bastion."

Jerry crosses his arms and begins tapping his foot nervously.

There's a card on the desk, in front of the video screens. Printed on it are the words:

SNAKE SANCTUARY CODE: 119

"Hey, we could always go to the Snake Sanctuary instead," you say. "Up to you."

"No way," Jerry says. "I'll take my chances with Project Fusion."

You nod. "Then let's go get those tranquilizers."

Head back outside *ON PAGE 126*

142

"You're right," you say. "I've been so focused on that big thing because it would be a grand gesture, really impress the Captain."

Jerry grips your shoulder. "Don't worry about it. Let's go get these animals under control!"

You drive the jeep down the path while Jerry stands in his seat, upper half through the sunroof, aiming his rifle ahead. A gazelle appears around a bend, eating some grass next to the road. You slow down enough for Jerry to aim and fire a dart. It catches the animal in the neck. The gazelle wavers and slowly falls to the grass.

"Nice shot!"

It's a safari hunt after that, Jerry shooting while you drive. A striped tiger appears along the path and Jerry takes it down before it can even react. Two giraffes are next, their long necks laying flat on the grass. Jerry is a surprisingly good marksman, hitting every single target. It's practically a game.

You must have subdued half the park by the time you reach the entrance. You skid to a stop and look up at your partner. "How many darts you got left?"

He checks the rack. "Just two. Huh. Didn't realize I had churned through that many."

You look around. The park seems much quieter now. There's still the other half that you haven't investigated, though. "Maybe we should go check out the Insect Enclosure," you say. "Or the Penguin Palace. You know, make sure they're all safe and closed up."

"Uhh," Jerry says. "What's that?"

There's a light coming in the distance. From the direction of the park entrance.

See what happens *ON PAGE 78*

143

The bushes part and a dark shape leaps out. You recoil in fear...

"Baaaah."

A goat stands in front of you, staring with round, innocent eyes. It cocks its head as if wondering why you're so scared.

"Baaaah!"

Two more goats wander into the clearing to say hello. They're completely unafraid.

Jerry gives you an embarrassed smirk.

"I broke my last dart," you say. "How many you got?"

"Just the one." He sighs. "We'd better make it count."

You pass a sign that says "Petting Zoo," which explains the goats. They follow you for the next ten minutes until you come to a gate, this one without a big padlock.

"Perfect." Jerry nods. "I can see the base of the Observation Tower just ahead."

Approach the Tower *ON PAGE 156*

144

You walk up to the rack of rifles. They stand almost as tall as you, with a carbon composite body and shiny barrel. Expensive. Why would a zoo need such fancy equipment?

Jerry reads your mind. "How often do the animals escape? I don't know why else they would be stocked like this..."

"Whatever the reason, we're glad they have them now." You grab the first rifle and sling it over your shoulder. "Do you see any ammo around here?"

Jerry opens a drawer and finds a box of darts. They're as long as your pointer finger, with a shiny steel needle on one end and colorful pink feathering on the other. "There are slots on the side of the gun to hold extra darts," Jerry explains. "One in the chamber, and three more on the side."

"So four each. You think that will be enough?"

"I don't see any other way to carry extra darts without accidentally poking ourselves."

Eight darts. It will have to be enough. "Now we just need to find Project Fusion, whatever it is. We'd better start looking."

Head back outside *ON PAGE 146*

145

Whether from memory or instinct, you select **Charcoal**.

A celebratory fanfare of horns blares out of a speaker in the podium. The screen flashes green.

Correct. Chewing on charcoal allows red colobus monkeys to eat potentially harmful foods, such as mango leaves and almonds, which contain toxins.

"Hey, nice job!" Jerry pats you on the back.

A small gold coin rolls out. You pick it up and examine it beneath your flashlight. "Observation Tower," you read, the letters printed around the outside of the coin.

"That's the tower at the center of the zoo," Jerry says.

"Maybe some other time," you say. "This doesn't help us get inside the Monkey Manor."

The monkeys hoot and cry, jumping up and down behind the bars.

YOU NOW HAVE THE TOWER TOKEN!

You don't have many options. *TURN TO PAGE 42*

146

You step out into the cool evening air just as another distant screech cuts through the rain. You and Jerry turn to follow the noise.

It's coming from the north. The forest directly ahead of you blocks most of the view, except for the Observation Tower standing over everything, a 300 foot tall needle above the treetops.

From the forest to the left you see a dark silhouette flapping into the sky. Its flight seems haphazard, abnormal. It screeches again and you get the distinct impression it's wounded. It reaches the top of the Observation Tower and lands.

"Looks like it found a good spot to build a nest," you say.

"That's definitely too high for us." Jerry nods to himself. "We'll just have to wait for the animal control specialists to get here to deal with *that*."

You stare at your partner. "We finally got our hands on some real weapons, and you want to call it quits?"

"No! I just don't think we should be going after that thing. You read the Zoo Announcement. It's dangerous."

"So what do you propose we do instead?"

He scratches the back of his neck. "We could stalk back to the entrance, sedating all the animals we see along the way. That's what we came here to do, right?"

You stare up at the Observation Tower and the dark figure perched there. Is it better to try and land one big prize, or a bunch of smaller ones?

To go to the Observation Tower, *HEAD TO PAGE 113*
To round up the other animals, *GO TO PAGE 161*

147

"That's easy. Everyone knows the most dangerous type of bear is the Grizzly." You press that answer on the screen and it flashes green with a fanfare of horns.

A gold coin rolls out into a tray. It says "Observation Tower" around the outside.

"Nice job dude," Jerry says.

You pocket the coin and turn away. "Don't call me dude. Now let's head back to the tower before it's too late!

It's tower time. *GO TO PAGE 154*

148

The jeep engine hums softly as you idle outside the Warden Hut. "Okay. So we have the tranquilizer rifles. Now what?"

Jerry looks in the glove compartment. There's a printed piece of paper inside. He clears his throat and reads:

ZOO ANNOUNCEMENT

Do not, I repeat, DO NOT, under any circumstances, approach Project Fusion within 50 feet. It moves extremely fast and without warning, so anything closer than that is too dangerous. Keep a wide range, guys. I mean it. Be safe.

-Warden Oxford

"Huh," Jerry says. "Looks like we shouldn't try to contain it after all."

You throw up your hands. "Are you kidding me, Jerry? All this time you've been whining about needing these tranquilizers, and now that we have them you want to give up?"

"I didn't say that! I just don't think we should go after Project Fusion. Even Warden Oxford says it's dangerous!" He shakes his head. "Instead, I think we should use these tranquilizers to round up the other animals in the park. Project Fusion is just one animal. It's a better use of our time to contain as many animals as possible."

Huh. You hadn't thought about that.

"You know I'm right," Jerry says. "Forget Project Fusion and let's focus on everything else. When we were on the roof I think I saw an elephant by the entrance!"

The Observation Tower looms in the distance, with the dark shape on the roof. What do you do?

To go to the Observation Tower, *DRIVE TO PAGE 129*

To round up the other animals, *GO TO PAGE 142*

149

POP.

The dart hisses through the air, pink feathers the only thing keeping it visible. You hold your breath as it arcs toward the Tower, toward the beast you were sent to subdue.

And falls short by twenty feet, clattering into the side of the tower.

"No!" Jerry cries, throwing down his rifle. "I thought I could reach it! I was certain!"

The shot disturbed the animal. It shifts as if turning to look down at you, though you can't make out any part of its body.

It screeches, a terrifying sound of fury.

Now what? *TURN TO PAGE 139*

150

You rush down the tower just as a line of black, windowless vans comes roaring into the clearing. One by one they halt at the base of the Observation Tower. You and Jerry share a look.

The door to the first van opens. You immediately recognize the two bars on the man's uniform. Indicating the rank of Captain.

You scramble forward and salute. "Captain Beckett, sir!"

Jerry is still standing there, holding the tranquilizer rifle. Only when you clear your throat does he jump next to you and mimic the salute.

Captain Beckett eyes the two of you. He's a bull of a man, sixty years old with broad shoulders and muscular arms. His uniform is tight and orderly, his face chiseled with discipline.

"Sir," you begin, "a status update. We have–"

He silences you with a hand and points up to the tower. "There was just an animal there. A *special* animal. What happened to it?"

You beam. "Jerry here hit it with a tranquilizer dart. It's out cold, sleeping on the roof."

Jerry places the barrel of the rifle on the ground to lean on it, smiling awkwardly.

Another man hops out of the passenger side of the first van. He looks like Teddy Roosevelt come alive: tan safari uniform, round spectacles, and reddish mustache.

"It's true? You've subdued Project–err, you've taken back control of my zoo?"

"It's okay," you say. "We know it's Project Fusion. We've seen the Zoo Announcements."

He squints suspiciously. "Then you saw the ones explaining just how dangerous it was? How you were to not get close, no matter what?"

You stand up straighter. "Yes, sir. But we knew we had to get close in order to get a good shot, regardless of the danger. And it worked."

For a moment he looks like he's going to explode. You brace yourself.

151

Warden Oxford breaks out into a big smile and sticks out his hand. "I'd like to shake the hand of the officer who has more guts than my zoo employees! Bunch of cowards, all of them. But not you. Oh no."

You shake his hand, then nod to Jerry. "He's the one who made the shot. I just stood there."

Oxford rushes over to clap Jerry on the shoulder. "Have you ever been on a safari, my boy?" He jumps into a story of the last time he was in Africa.

Captain Beckett looks at you, hands clasped behind his back. Judging you.

"Captain, I know we didn't get the *entire* zoo under control, but we did our best. We've secured half the park, and based on all the Zoo Announcements it was clear this was the most important–"

"Corporal Rodriguez," he interrupts, "you need to quit while you're ahead."

"Sir?"

He finally breaks into a big smile. "You've done a phenomenal job here. Much better than I expected, no offense. I didn't think anyone could get this place under control, not even my best officer."

"You think I'm you're best officer?"

"I *know* you are! And this only proves it. Especially in victory, giving Jerry all of the credit. A good officer deflects all praise and accepts all responsibility."

You give one final glance back toward the top of the tower, wondering what the animal was. Maybe someday you'll find out. "Thank you, sir."

He wraps an arm around your shoulder and leads you away. "Now, about that Lieutenant promotion. I'm going to draw up the paperwork tomorrow. I want you to start immediately. If you're up for it, of course."

"Sir. After tonight, I'm up for anything!"

THE END

152

You take a quick look around the roof. There's not much there, just some air conditioning units and a lip around the edge. "Come on up Jerry," you whisper down.

He seems reluctant, but obeys. You pull him up the final few steps.

Another screech in the distance makes you jump, and you very nearly fall off the roof. You and Jerry turn to follow the noise.

It's coming from the north. Up on the roof you have a wonderful view of the park, with the tops of buildings sticking out above the trees in all directions. The Observation Tower stands over everything, a 300 foot tall needle.

From the forest to the left you see a dark silhouette flapping into the sky. Its flight seems haphazard, abnormal. It screeches again and you get the distinct impression it's wounded. It reaches the top of the Observation Tower and lands.

"Looks like it found a good spot to build a nest," you say.

"That's definitely too high for us." Jerry nods to himself. "We'll just have to wait for the animal control specialists to get here to deal with *that*."

"We'll see." You look around. "Looks like there's a vent over there. I bet we can get inside through that."

Investigate the vent *ON PAGE 155*

153

You nod to Jerry, an unspoken signal among long-time partners. Both of you count to three in your heads.

POP POP.

Two darts whiz toward the hyenas. And two hyenas stumble backwards, teeter for a moment, and then slump to the ground.

You don't waste time celebrating. While the remaining two hyenas look at their sleeping comrades, you and Jerry quickly reload your tranquilizer rifles. You raise your rifle to your shoulder and squeeze the trigger.

The third hyena lays down on the grass and closes its eyes.

Jerry's shot comes a moment later, pacifying the fourth hyena. All of them sit along the side of the road in a line, like sleeping babies in a nursery.

"That was lucky," you say.

Jerry stands proudly. "Nothing lucky about it. At least not for me. You, on the other hand..."

You laugh, but cut off as you glance at your gun. "I'm out of darts."

"I've still got one," Jerry says. "I guess we'd better make it count."

The Observation Tower looms above. "Come on. We're almost to the base of the Tower."

Approach the Tower *ON PAGE 156*

154

You step inside the lobby of the tower. It's not very large. There's a door to the elevator in front of you, and a stairwell on the side.

Jerry approaches the elevator and presses the button. Nothing happens.

"Guess we're taking the stairs, huh?"

You have a strange sense of foreboding as you climb the tower's many steps. It feels like you're marching to war, even though Jerry is the only one with a tranquilizer rifle now. He's silent too, so he must be feeling the same thing.

After what feels like an hour, but was probably just ten minutes, you reach the observation deck. It's an open balcony that runs 360 degrees around the tower. From there you should have a good view of the Project Fusion animal on the roof.

You remain in the doorway. "Ready to head out there?"

"Let me catch my breath first."

"You're not scared, are you Jerry?"

He looks at you with shock. "Dude, of course I'm scared. I'm *terrified.*"

For once you don't tell him not to call you that.

Head out to the deck *ON PAGE 100*

155

The vent comes away easily, revealing a ladder. "Well look at that. Easy."

Jerry says nothing.

You climb down the ladder into a large, dark room. You get the sense that the blackness is hiding something, but can't tell what. Your feet hit the ground at the bottom and you feel around the wall with your hands. They touch something that feels like a light switch. Saying a quick prayer, you flip it.

The lights overhead come on, suddenly blinding you. Jerry is halfway down the ladder and yelps.

"Sorry!"

As he finishes his descent you realize you're in a garage. And sure enough, there's a big jeep in the center of the room. Not only that, but the jeep has a gun rack mounted on the side, with two long guns...

"Tranquilizer rifles!"

You run to the side and hold one of the guns in your hand. It looks like any normal rifle except for the fuzzy dart in the chamber. There's a bandoleer with five more darts on it, and you throw it over your shoulder.

Jerry has a big smile on his face as he approaches. "Finally, some real firepower."

You put the rifle back and hop into the jeep. The keys are in the ignition. Jerry opens the garage door and you drive out into the forest, finally feeling like you're prepared for whatever may come.

You've got the tranquilizers! Now figure out what to do *ON PAGE 148*

156

The path opens up to a clearing, with the huge Observation Tower ahead. You stop to gaze up at it. It's like a big water tower, but with an observation deck at the top. Above that is the roof, where the Project Fusion beast has made its home.

"So... now what?" Jerry asks.

It's tough to tell from so far away, but it appears that the animal is leaning over the edge of the roof. You watch for a long moment and then nod. "You can see part of it. Just above the observation deck."

Jerry cranes his head. "Yeah, I think you're right."

"Can you hit it from here?"

A long silence stretches.

"Maybe," he finally says. "I think so. Yeah."

You snort. "Well which is it?"

"Maybe a fifty-fifty shot."

You look at the door at the base of the Tower. "We could always climb inside. Get closer."

"Yeah, maybe. I wish I had more darts..."

But you *don't* have more darts. So you're going to have to decide.

To trust Jerry's aim and shoot, *GO TO PAGE 127*

To try getting closer, *ADVANCE TO PAGE 134*

157

"Plastic sounds like the right answer," you say. "Unless you've got a better guess."

"Nope. I have no idea."

You select **Plastic**. A horn inside the podium beeps, and the screen flashes red.

The correct answer was **Charcoal**. *Chewing on charcoal allows red colobus monkeys to eat potentially harmful foods, such as mango leaves and almonds, which contain toxins.*

"How were we supposed to know that?" Jerry complains. "That's not fair at all."

You shrug. "Maybe we'll get another chance later. Either way, it doesn't help us get inside this Monkey Manor."

The monkeys hoot and cry, jumping up and down behind the bars.

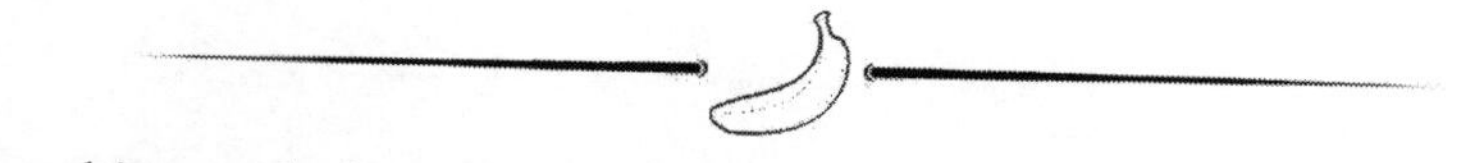

There's nothing to do but *TURN TO PAGE 42*

158

POP.

The dart hisses through the air, pink feathers the only thing keeping it visible. You hold your breath as it arcs toward the Tower, toward the beast you were sent to subdue.

And strikes the animal.

"Yes!" Jerry cries, hoisting his rifle in the air in victory. "I knew I could hit it!"

But then the pink blur starts drifting back toward the ground. You and Jerry barely jump out of the way as it strikes the ground, needle-first.

You run over to examine the dart. There's dirt around the tip of the needle, but nothing else. It appears to still be full of sedative.

"It bounced off," you whisper. "It didn't stick!"

The shot has disturbed the animal. It shifts as if turning to look down at you, though you can't make out any part of its body.

It screeches, a terrifying sound of fury.

Now what? *TURN TO PAGE 139*

159

Something stops you. You reach up and grab the barrel of the rifle and lower it.

"Rodriguez?"

"We have this token," you say, fishing it out of your pocket.

"Don't even *think* about suggesting what I think you're about to suggest."

You look up at the dark shape on the roof. "Jerry, there's something about the animal. I think... I think it's wounded."

"Well yeah. It looked wounded when it flew up here. But wounded animals are the most dangerous kind!"

You grip his arm insistently. "Jerry, I'm telling you. I don't think it's dangerous."

He shakes his head. "No. No way. This is madness, Rodriguez. I'm not letting you..."

Before he can finish you're walking across the roof.

"Rodriguez," he hisses, trying to yell and remain quiet at the same time. "Rodriguez!"

The token fits in a coin slot on the gate. "Cover me from there!" you whisper back.

Jerry grumbles something but raises the rifle, watching.

The gate opens. The stairs beckon you up into the sky.

I hope you know what you're doing. Climb to the roof *ON PAGE 84*

160

The Warden Hut is a nondescript cement building with a flat roof, sort of like a bunker. There's a larger door on the side to a garage of some kind. The entire structure looks like it could withstand a bomb blast.

You approach the main door. It's metal and electronic, far more elaborate than something you'd expect to find at a zoo. And more intimidating than any of the other zoo doors so far.

"There's a keycode entry," you say. "We haven't gotten the code for this place, have we?"

Your partner shakes his head.

Now that the park power is restored, the building is illuminated on all sides by big floodlights. You walk around the structure until you come to a ladder on the side. It leads up to the roof two stories above.

"We could see if there's a way in up there," you say.

Jerry cocks his head. "I don't know. It doesn't look too safe. See that huge gash in the wall, there?"

Halfway up the building there's a rend in the cement five feet long, crossing over the ladder. Like a massive claw raked across the side. Some of the cement underneath the ladder is crumbling.

"I'll go first," you decide. "And you'll wait until I'm all the way up before following." Before Jerry can protest, you begin climbing.

You take the rungs one at a time, the sound of boots on metal ringing louder than you would like in the forest. The ladder is wobbly around the broken area, but with just one person it bears your weight fine.

Check out the roof *ON PAGE 152*

161

"You're right," you say. "I've been so focused on that big thing because it would be a grand gesture, really impress the Captain."

Jerry grips your shoulder. "Don't worry about it. Let's go get these animals under control!"

You jog along the path with the rifles held across your chest. A gazelle appears around a bend, eating some grass next to the road. Jerry takes aim and fires a dart. It catches the animal in the neck. The gazelle wavers and slowly falls to the grass.

"Nice shot!"

It's a safari hunt after that, running along and putting a dart in every animal you come across. A striped tiger appears along the path and Jerry takes it down before it can even react. Two giraffes are next, their long necks laying flat on the grass. You hit one and Jerry nabs the other. Jerry is a surprisingly good marksman, hitting every single target. It's practically a game.

You must have subdued half the park by the time you reach the entrance. You skid to a stop and look at your partner. "How many darts you got left?"

"Just one. Huh. Didn't realize I had churned through that many."

"Same here." You look around. The park seems much quieter now. There's still the other half that you haven't investigated, though. "Maybe we should go check out the Insect Enclosure," you say. "Or the Penguin Palace. You know, make sure they're all safe and closed up."

"Uhh," Jerry says. "What's that?"

There's a light coming in the distance. From the direction of the park entrance.

See what happens *ON PAGE 78*

162

"I think the answer might be Aluminum," you say.

"I have no idea, so I trust your gut."

You select **Aluminum**. A horn inside the podium beeps, and the screen flashes red.

The correct answer was ***Charcoal****. Chewing on charcoal allows red colobus monkeys to eat potentially harmful foods, such as mango leaves and almonds, which contain toxins.*

"That's not fair at all," Jerry complains. "How were we supposed to know the answer to such an obscure question?"

You shrug. "Maybe we'll get another chance later. Either way, it doesn't help us get inside this Monkey Manor."

The monkeys hoot and cry, jumping up and down behind the bars.

HEAD BACK TO PAGE 42

163

You think the answer is Black Bear, so that's what you press. The podium flashes red and makes a decidedly angry beeping noise. Incorrect.

"Aww man," Jerry says.

Feeling awful for getting it wrong, you return to the observation railing. The gold coin taunts you. So close, yet so far away.

"Find some rope," you call to Jerry. "I'm going in."

"Wait!"

You start to climb, but Jerry runs up and grabs your arm. "No way. *No way.* You're not going in there. You would immediately regret that decision."

"But we need that coin!"

Jerry shakes his head. "No we don't. We can still climb pretty high in the tower, we just won't be able to get to the roof. We shouldn't get *that* close anyways. You read the note."

A bear comes strolling out of the cave below, slow and lazy. It looks up at you as if wondering what all the commotion is about.

Jerry glares at you. "See? I told you that would have been a bad idea!"

Seeing the bear shakes you out of it. "Yeah, you're right. Okay. Let's head back to the tower then."

Jerry nods as if you've finally come to your senses.

Head back into the tower *ON PAGE 154*

164

"It's a good thing I remember this." You press the button for **Coral Snake.**

The screen flashes green and some trumpets play. A gold coin rolls out of the side and into a small tray.

"No thanks to you, Jerry."

He's still looking around nervously. "Good for you, partner. I knew you'd get it. Now let's get out of here, okay?"

YOU NOW HAVE THE TOWER TOKEN!

Make your way back to the tower *ON PAGE 154*

165

"Do it," you whisper.

Jerry doesn't hesitate. With a loud hiss the dart shoots forward, pink feathering sticking out of the dark animal.

It roars, a terrible, angry sound.

It turns toward you. Yellow eyes glow in the night. It takes a step forward but stumbles, losing its balance. It falls forward and lands with its head hanging over the roof, eyes closed.

Unconscious.

"We did it!" you yell, high-fiving Jerry. "Nice shot, dude!"

He grins from ear to ear. "Don't call me dude!"

You approach the edge of the roof where the animal's head hangs. It's the only body part you can see, but it's clearly a bird's head, although it's the size of a big beach ball, with eyes as round as saucers. "Told you it was a bird," Jerry says. "I mean, it was obvious since it could fly, but still."

It seems so peaceful in sleep. You could have sworn there was more to it than that, but you guess it was just a really big bird all along. "Maybe we can find a way up to the roof to get a better look," you say. "After all this trouble I want to see..."

The sound of car engines drifts up from the ground. You and Jerry return to the railing in time to see a line of headlights snaking through the forest, coming your way.

"Just in time," you say. "Let's go brag about what we've done."

Head downstairs *ON PAGE 150*

166

You grab Jerry before he can raise the rifle. "Come on!"

"But..."

"*COME ON!*"

He allows himself to be dragged away, and the two of you sprint down a side path into the woods. After a hundred feet you hear the sound of laughing behind you, the hyenas following. Stalking. You dare not look back.

The path is barely more than some mud and gravel, and you nearly lose your footing several times. It's not easy sprinting for your life while carrying a long rifle!

"Where does this path lead?" Jerry asks.

"I don't know. Hopefully someplace safe!"

"Hopefully!"

Cross your fingers *ON PAGE 93*

167

Just as the spider's hairy leg brushes against your pants, a paralyzing sound cuts the air, like a dog whistle but more electronic. You clutch your ears and roll onto your side. It feels like someone is drilling into your ears!

Through clenched eyes you notice the two remaining spiders are trembling. One of them takes a step back, teetering as if drunk. The other follows in the same condition. They stumble that way across the room and into one of the broken glass enclosures.

The sound cuts out and Jerry appears next to you. He lowers a hand. "Dude, I told you to not to move!"

You gratefully let him pull you to your feet. "Hey, *you* try playing chicken against a bunch of giant spiders. And stop calling me dude!"

He laughs and holds out his other hand. There's a small oval device in his palm, like a garage door opener. "This it was on the wall inside. Subsonic interference device. Used it just in time!"

"Just in time," you agree. "Was there anything else in the office?"

He shrugs. "I didn't have much time to check. I was too busy saving your butt." He looks over his shoulder. "Want to go back and look around? If those spiders come back..."

You don't even have to think about it. "Nope. I don't know what else is in this zoo, but we need some better weapons. Let's go get those tranquilizer rifles."

Head back outside *ON PAGE 75*

SNEAK PEEK

Welcome to the Aurora Hotel!

You are SCOTT REINHART, an invited guest on this snowy Saturday night. An icy wind ushers you up the steps, through the threshold and into the magnificent Grand Lobby. It's your first time here since your uncle Gus bought the place. Unfortunately you heard it hasn't been doing well. The turn-of-last-century hotel has a long history, and none of it good. You've read reports of freak accidents, of guests disappearing, even tales that the place is haunted! In fact–

"Scotty!"

You trip over your duffel bag as you're nearly tackled to the marble floor. When you look up it's into the smiling face of your cousin Jenna. Over her shoulder, grinning apologetically, is your other cousin – her twin brother Evan.

"You made it!"

You can't help but laugh. "Of course I made it!" Their email came more than a week ago. Something about them needing help. Something about being able to help your uncle Gus, too. Casually you glance around for him. Except for a few scattered guests, the hotel looks pretty empty.

"Come upstairs," Evan says. "Our rooms are all ready. We can tell you everything."

A half hour later you're all settled in. You and Evan are sharing a room, with Jenna's connected via an adjoining door. Your cousins have been here for a few days, you realize. Since before the snows started to fall. Silently you envy them for missing out on a few days of school.

"So what's this about?" you ask. "Something about... a letter?"

The twins look at each other. Evan reaches into his pocket and pulls out a folded piece of tattered, yellowed paper. The handwriting on it is barely legible.

170

My preparations have been meticulous. The ceremony is arranged.

Alone I have gathered all four artifacts that are somehow still bound to this place. With them I can close the nether-gate -- on this night of all nights -- and restore peace to the Aurora Hotel.

I can only pray that all goes well. That he does not show himself, or interfere in any way.

By tomorrow it will all be over. One way or another.

-- Alastair Roakes   All Hallows Eve, 1909

"Whoa," you say. "Where in the world did you *find* this?"

"In a hidden compartment," Evan replies, "of some antique desk that's bounced its way around the hotel."

"And that's not all," Jenna adds. "There was a photo tucked away with it. An *old* photo."

171

"Is that him?" you ask. "This... Alastair guy?"

The twins nod in unison. "We guess so," Jenna says. "I mean, that's what we're counting on, anyway."

172

Jenna casts her brother a concerned look. "Evan, tell him."

Your cousin looks uncomfortable. Then again, he usually does. Evan's the smartest guy you know, but he was never good with people. Or words. "Things are bad here," he begins. "Something is... well, something is *wrong* with this place."

"What do you mean by wrong?"

He pauses, searching for the right words. "My father is worried, Scott. When he bought this place he got it cheap, so he knew something was probably up. But he always thought it was something he could fix. Some new plaster here, some fresh paint there – that sort of thing. Hey, the place is old. It's expected. Only the longer we stay here, the weirder it gets."

"Not weird, haunted!" Jenna cries. You can tell your more vociferous cousin was a having a hard time keeping silent. "This place is creepy, cuz. People have seen things. *We've* seen things. It's driving the customers away and making things miserable for dad."

You blink. So that's why the hotel seems practically empty. But *haunted*? For some reason it doesn't make sense. For Jenna to be convinced, maybe, but Evan has always been the more rational of the two.

"So what can *I* do?" you ask. "Why'd you call me up here?"

Evan holds up the letter. "Four artifacts," he reads. He points to the photograph. "Now look on the table. A bell, a candle, a crystal ball–"

"–and a book," Jenna adds. "Don't forget about the book."

You study the photo. The man seated at the table certainly *appears* like he's about to conduct some sort of ceremony. The four strange artifacts lay spread out before him. *An arrangement*, you think quietly.

"Let's say this is Alastair," you offer. "So what? This guy is long gone. The ceremony is long since over."

"Not if he never finished it," Jenna says. Her eyes sparkle with a strange excitement. "Think about it, Scotty. This guy Alastair knew the hotel was haunted. His ceremony was meant to put it at rest. Only it's *not* at rest, which means whatever he was trying to do didn't work. He failed, or–"

"– or he got interrupted," Evan finishes. "See what it says? Hopefully 'he' won't show himself. So who is 'he'? And what if he *did* show himself?"

173

Evan pauses. "A long time ago, there was a big explosion here, in the basement of the hotel. We looked it up. Know when it was?"

"1909?"

"Yes. Halloween night. Or all Hallows' Eve, depending on how you phrase it." Your cousin's eyes narrow. You've never seen him this focused. "We're thinking this 'he' showed up. Messed up Alastair's plans."

"There's a pile of guest logs in the old storage room," Jenna goes on. "The records say an Alastair Roakes checked into the Aurora a few days before the explosion. But he never paid his bill. He never checked out."

You let loose a broken chuckle. "Think he's still here?" When you look up though, your cousins aren't laughing.

"This '*he*' guy might still be here," Evan shrugs. "Might even be the bad guy people keep seeing around. Maybe he's the one responsible for this 'nethergate' in the first place."

Bad guy? You decide not to ask. "So what's the plan?"

"Simple," Jenna says. "We search the Aurora top to bottom for these four objects. When we've gathered them all, maybe we can somehow finish the ceremony."

"And close the nethergate," Evan adds. "Solve the whole ghost problem here, once and for all."

You nod. Seems simple enough. Too simple, actually. "The bell, candle, crystal and book... wouldn't these things be long gone by now?"

"Not if they were *bound* to this place," Evan answers. "Like it says here in the letter."

A smile crosses your face, mirroring Jenna's. "Sure, why not? I'm in!" Your cousins' enthusiasm is rubbing off on you. "But how are we going to search this place while guests are here? Won't uncle Gus – I mean your dad – come down on us?"

"That's why we wait until midnight," Jenna says. "Most of the hotel will be shut down. We'll have free run of the place!"

"Plus," Evan adds, "after midnight the date will be right too. It'll be All Hallows' Eve..."

174

A few hours and a couple of cheeseburgers later (courtesy of Uncle Gus!) you're still relaxing in your room. Despite everyone agreeing to try and get some rest, you're just too excited to sleep tonight. Still, your eyes are getting heavy when suddenly–

"Happy Halloween!" Jenna bursts through your suite door like a kid on Christmas morning. It's not even two seconds after midnight. "You guys ready?'

"Yeah..." Evan groans as he sits up. "In a few."

As Jenna bounces over you notice she's holding something. "What's that?"

"I swiped the master key from the front desk," she declares proudly. Your cousin shakes a piece of paper in her other hand. "And the guest manifest, too. That way we can tell which rooms are empty."

"Nice!" You squint curiously at the large bronze key Jenna is spinning around the tip of her finger. "Wow, they still use *keys* here?"

"It's an old hotel," Evan explains. "It's all part of the charm."

Jenna chuckles. "You sound like dad, trying to save money." She flops onto the bed. "Okay, we only have until morning. 42 rooms, three floors... this place is big. Evan and I already decided we're gonna need to split up."

175

Evan swipes the key mid-spin, then takes a copy of the manifest from his sister. "I'll take this level. The first floor. See what I can find."

"And I'll start at the lobby level," Jenna says. "There's lots of stuff to check out downstairs."

"Once we're done, we can meet up at the elevator," Evan says. "Then we can all do the second floor together. Cool?"

"Cool!" cries Jenna. She whirls to face you. "So Scotty... the big question: Who you goin' with?"

Who will you follow when you explore...

THE SECRET OF THE AURORA HOTEL

ABOUT THE AUTHORS

David Kristoph lives in Virginia with his wonderful wife and two not-quite German Shepherds. He's a fantastic reader, great videogamer, good chess player, average cyclist, and mediocre runner. He's also a member of the Planetary Society, patron of StarTalk Radio, amateur astronomer and general space enthusiast. He writes mostly Science Fiction and Fantasy. www.DavidKristoph.com

Danny McAleese started writing fantasy fiction during the golden age of Dungeons & Dragons, way back in the heady, adventure-filled days of the 1980's. His short stories, The Exit, and Momentum, made him the Grand Prize winner of Blizzard Entertainment's 2011 Global Fiction Writing contest.

He currently lives in NY, along with his wife, four children, three dogs, and a whole lot of chaos. www.dannymcaleese.com

WANT THIS BOOKMARK?

Review any one of our
Ultimate Ending books on Amazon
and we'll mail you a
glossy, full-color version!

Just send a screenshot
of your review to:
Bookmark@UltimateEndingBooks.com
and don't forget to include
your mailing address.

That's it!

(And thank you!)

NOTES

NOTES

Made in the USA
Lexington, KY
24 July 2017